The Neighborhood

Debbie Williams

BIGfamily Publishing

Copyright © 2020 by BIGfamily Publishing. All rights reserved

The characters and events portrayed in this book are fictitious. Any similarity to real persons, living or dead, is coincidental and not intended by the author.

No part of this book may be reproduced, or stored in a retrieval system, or transmitted in any form or by any means, electronic, mechanical, photocopying, recording, or otherwise, without express written permission of the publisher.

ISBN: 9798642955109

Cover design by: Sara Hanna
Library of Congress Control Number: 2018675309
Published in the United States BIGfamily Publishing

All rights reserved.

DEDICATION

To Jeff, you still make me smile inside and out.

ACKNOWLEDGMENTS

My warmest thank you to the friends and family who provided support and encouragement on this new chapter in my life. A special thanks to Rob and Ann for Sunday night chats and being there from the beginning as well as all my friends and family who offered feedback through the re-write process. A big thanks to my daughter, Lauren, for her invaluable support in helping me to fine-tune the story and in editing (after all who doesn't want a chance to edit their mother). I'm grateful to my talented daughter, Sara, for providing the graphics for the book and to my son, Colin, for his long-distance support. I was blessed with a wonderful mother and mother-in-law who were great encouragers and I know they are with me in spirit. Lastly, I'd like to thank my husband, Jeff. No one could ask for a more supporting and loving partner to share their life with. You are my Peter.

The Neighborhood

Debbie Williams

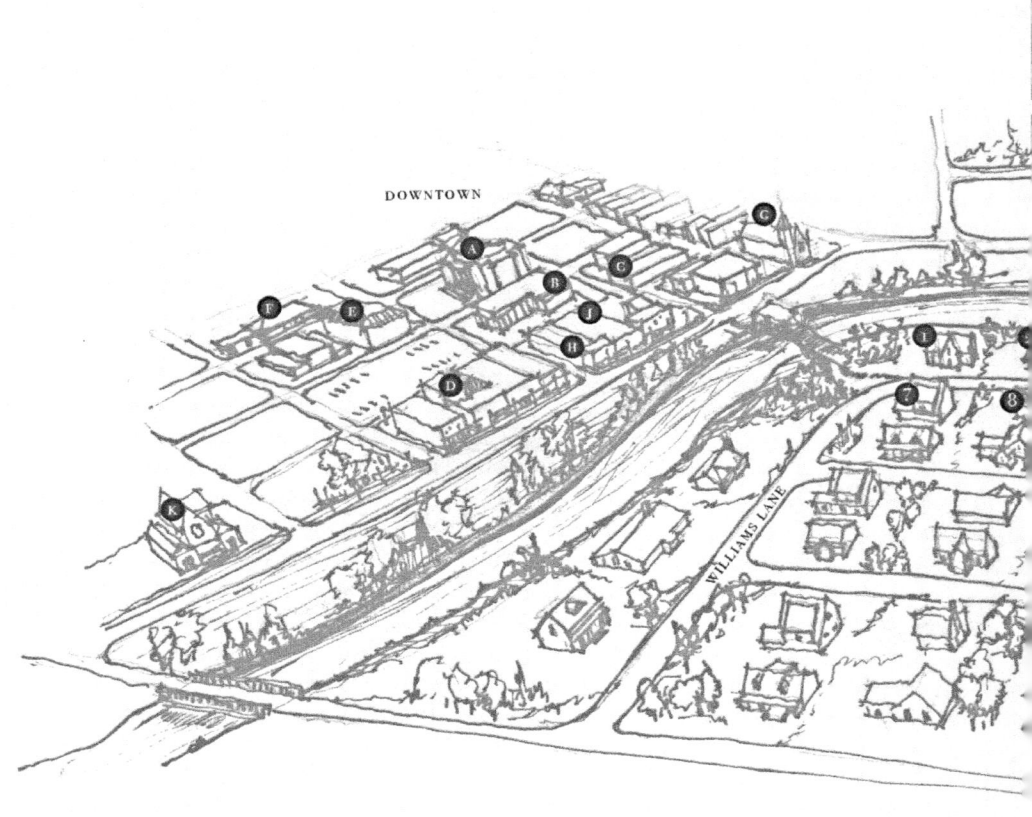

- (A) PERFORMING ARTS CENTER
- (B) RESTAURANT
- (C) WINE BAR
- (D) SANDWICH SHOP
- (E) POST OFFICE
- (F) BANK
- (G) METHODIST CHURCH
- (H) COFFEE SHOP
- (J) BOOKSTORE
- (K) PRESBYTERIAN CHURCH
- (L) LIBRARY
- (M) WELCOME CENTER
- (N) GRAD SCHOOL
- (O) BUSINESS
- (P) ARTS & SCIENCE
- (Q) STUDENT CENTER
- (R) J.R. WHITELY RESEARCH CENTER
- (S) HEALTH SCIENCES
- (T) CENTER OF GLOBAL EDUCATION
- (U) ADMINISTRATION

The Neighborhood

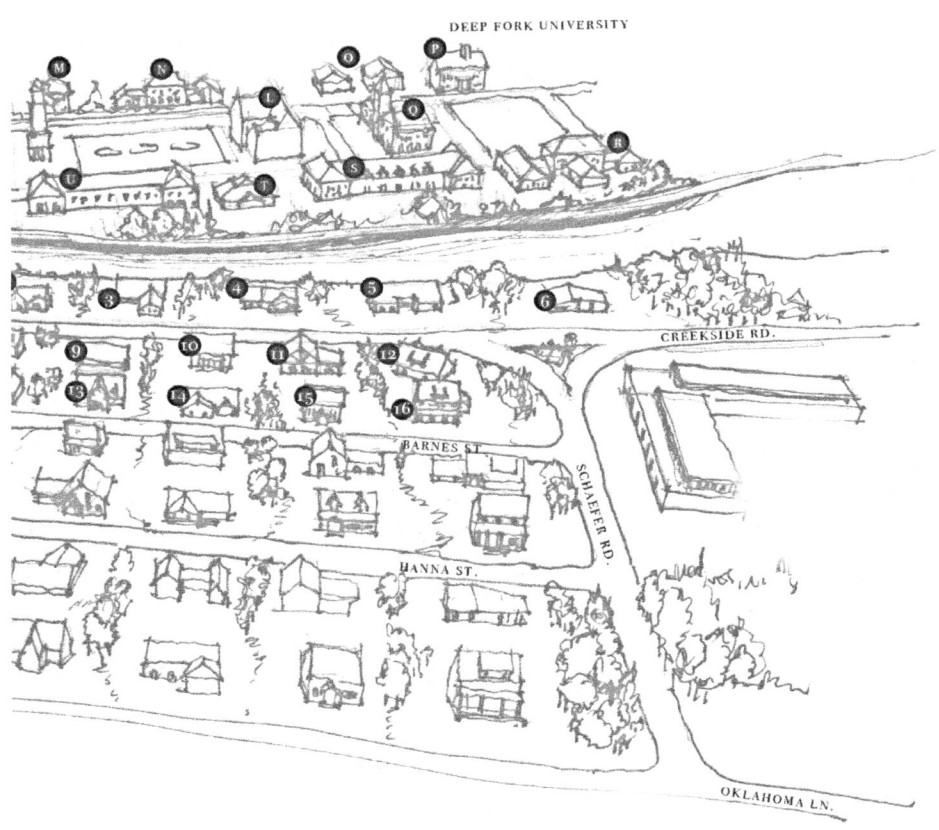

1. GARY BARRETT & SOFIA GOMEZ
2. ALAN & TRACEY MARSHALL
3. BOB & BETTY JOHNSON † CORNELIUS
4. RANDALL & JEAN WEBER † MILLIE
5. PHILILP & ANN ANDREWS
6. KEVIN CRANK
7. ARNOLD & LYNDA THOMAS
8. KEITH & ADRIANNA HOLDEN
9. JAKE & DIANE THORNE
10. BILL & JO WALKER
11. EVELYN & PETER JOHNS
12. MANASI & KAMYA PATEL
13. MISS ESSIE
14. MATTHEW, LAUREN, EMMA & HANNAH BARNES
15. VICTOR & CYNTHIA ANDERSON
16. JIN & MIN JUNG

Chapter 1

"I hope the cat's okay" is all I could think as I scurried across the street to the Johnson's house. Ever since the couple had retired, it felt as if they were off traveling more than they were home. A great way to spend retirement and I didn't mind checking on Cornelius, but with the holidays and all, I'd been chasing my own tail as well as the cat's. A few days ago, when I'd stopped by, there was no sign of the persnickety feline. Not unusual, but always a bit unsettling. Stepping into the laundry room, I was relieved to see the food dish nearly empty. Out of the corner of my eye, I saw a streak as Cornelius ran under the couch. Ours was not a close relationship. I was merely a means to an end for Cornelius - survival. At least when Betty texted me today for her Cornelius update, I could honestly say he seemed pleased to see me.

My cell phone rang as I was refilling the water and food bowls. Seeing Peter's name appear on the screen, I answered immediately. "Hi, Ev." I always smile when I hear him say Ev. Peter is the only person in my entire life to shorten my name, and I love it. Not one for pet names, this was as good as I was going to get from my husband.

"Just leaving the office. Do you need me to pick up anything for this evening?" I ticked off the last items we would need for the evening's party, hung up and finished my Cornelius chores.

Walking across the street to my house, I inhaled deeply. Although it was the beginning of January, the temperature was in the mid 50's, the sun was shining and there was no wind, which is somewhat unusual in Oklahoma. I calculated if I would have enough time to take a walk around the block before final preparations for the evening and determined the answer was definitely a yes. I love walking through my neighborhood. Most of the houses were built between the two world wars coinciding with Oklahoma's oil boom. The variety of architecture our neighborhood offered appealed to both my architectural historian husband's interests and mine. Within a four-block radius, one could find Tudor style bungalows, Craftsman cottages, Spanish revival homes and the influence of the Art Deco movement. Side by side still stand modest homes and what once were considered mansions. No matter the size of the house, almost everyone enjoyed a large lawn and trees that have stood since before the depression. There were a few houses built after the 1940's, but not many.

Preparing to turn the corner, I glanced at the Crank house. Lane used to call it the "Cranky" house. A later addition to our block, it was built in the late 1950's by George and Ethel Crank. It definitely did not fit into the vernacular of the neighborhood. The low-pitched roof and simple lines created what was considered a modern look in our quite traditional neighborhood. Some even considered it an eye sore. The Cranks passed away a few years before we moved into the neighborhood, leaving the house to a nephew and subsequently to his children. For the past twenty years, it had been a rental, sometimes even committing the cardinal sin of leasing to college students. Definitely a source of irritation in the neighborhood! A few months ago, the great, great nephew of the original owner moved in and started a renovation of the house.

Picking up the pace, I looped the block and saw my daughter crossing the bridge that connects our neighborhood to downtown Deep Fork. Unlike many towns whose founding neighborhoods eventually fell into decline, ours has stayed a very desirable place to live. The creek, which borders the houses on two sides, separates the neighborhood from the town center on the west and from the local university on the north. A pedestrian bridge connects the neighborhood to the downtown and serves as a gateway to restaurants, coffee shops and stores. The fact that the town center is within walking distance of Deep Fork University has helped to keep the area vibrant as well. The partnerships created between the city and DFU were mutually beneficial. The joint enterprise to renovate the Carnegie Library into a performing arts center not only provided cultural opportunities but also helped support local restaurants. When DFU purchased some vacant warehouses and renovated them for student housing, the downtown really exploded.

As Lane approached, I once again said a prayer of thanksgiving for such a beautiful daughter. Although physically lovely, her beauty really shines through her kind heart and quick smile. If eyes are a window to the soul then Lane's would be akin to a large picture window. She has experienced joy and deep sorrow in her quarter of a century of life. Generally, I read her emotional status within seconds of peering into her eyes. Today I saw contentment and happiness.

"How was your coffee with Sara?" I asked as Lane joined me.

"Great! She loves living in Savannah and has met a guy she's crazy about. He's a musician, which matches her artistic soul. They've only been dating a few months so we'll see. I invited her to stop by tonight."

"Perfect! I'd love to see her. I've always enjoyed Sara. She always has an interesting perspective on life," I said with a wink. Lane and Sara had been friends since they were seven years old. Lane is the yang to Sara's ying. Sara is free-spirited and spontaneous. Lane is grounded, a planner and likes to keep pro/con lists. The two could not be more different, yet their friendship has stood the test of time. "Speaking of tonight, I could use some help with last-minute preparations."

"Sure" Lane replied, "just let me send a few e-mails, then I'm all yours." As we walked up to the house, I couldn't help but smile. Lane was happy. What more could a mother want? After graduating from Oklahoma State University with a marketing degree, she moved to Dallas to work with a travel company. At an early age she had caught the "travel bug" from her dad and me so this was a natural fit. The job allowed her to work offsite when she wanted, which meant she periodically set up camp with us. Ultimately, her goal was to save enough money to take a year and travel. If you asked Lane what I thought about this plan, she would tell you I think it will be a great adventure. The truth is it scares the bejeebers out of me. I believe it is my inalienable right as a mother to worry. I can't help but think of all the things that can go wrong for a young woman traveling alone.

Peter pulled up just as Lane and I reached the front porch. Ours was definitely not one of the larger homes in the neighborhood, but it was perfect for the three of us. The Tudor style home was built in the 1930's. Ten years ago, we did an extensive remodel of the interior, expanding our bedroom and adding a master bathroom. We also updated the kitchen, created a more open floor plan and added a covered porch off the rear of the house. Other than routine maintenance, the exterior stayed true to its original architecture. The front porch was the first thing that drew me to this house. The brick archway that frames the entryway is cozy and inviting, a great place to visit with a neighbor, read a book or just contemplate life.

Lane went to help her dad carry in the groceries while I put away the key to the Johnson's house. On the inside of the broom closet door is a series of key racks. The top one is for personal keys (cars, house…). The next three racks hold "The Neighborhood" keys. As in most neighborhoods, you leave a key with a neighbor for when you are traveling or for an emergency. Over the twenty years we've lived in the neighborhood, I've accumulated quite a collection. In some cases, I have keys from one or two previous owners of a house. Peter teases me that we could supplement our retirement income by becoming burglars. After all who would

...rhood

...nd tasks assigned, the three of
...dy for the evening's get
...ying to host a holiday party
...years ago, we began our
...;. As a lifelong Methodist, I
...ıristmas through Epiphany
...ly comfortable leaving up my
...ends and family to join us after
...ided a bit.

Before changing for the evening, I did a quick walk through of the house. I love my home. There is absolutely nothing pretentious about it. A couch built for comfort and oversized chairs lent themselves to evenings of reading and watching television. My mainstays for decorating are family photos and books. The warm grays and muted tones looked especially good with the reds and greens of the holiday decorations. Not overly decorated, it just feels comfortable. Peter had once said, "It's soft in all the right places, just like you, Ev." I hadn't talked to him for three days after that comment. But he was right. I was never one of those tall, long limbed athletic types but more of an average height, with the shape of a pear. That changed thanks to menopause. Now I carried a pudginess around my waist which encourages me to seek out stretchable pants. Without being self-deprecating I would not describe myself as a beauty. I've always thought if I were cast in a movie, rather than playing the gorgeous heroine, I would play the loveable best friend. Which was fine, I am rarely comfortable being in the limelight, I'd much rather be the wingman.

If there's nothing pretentious about our house, then there's definitely nothing grandiose in how we dress! Again, comfort is what we're all about. I think Peter has basically worn the same outfit since I met him thirty years ago. Jeans and a white shirt. If he wants to dress up, he might wear a black shirt, have the jeans starched and MAYBE add a sport coat. In colder weather, he might don a fleece vest.

Debbie Williams

I can't say my wardrobe has much more diversity. I tend to wear basic colors: black, navy, beiges. Occasionally, I'll add a pink or shades of blue. Every time I try to add bright colors, I feel like my clothes are arriving ahead of me. Tunic tops and jeans (with lycra of course) make up the majority of my wardrobe. I'm in a rut, but I'm okay with that. If I'm talking to my sister about going to an event she'll say "Let me guess, you're wearing your dark wash jeans, a black tunic and silver hoop earrings." I'd say she's spot on about 90% of the time. For tonight's party I stayed with my standard outfit but decided to accessorize with gold jewelry.

I took a quick shower and blew dry my shoulder length blonde hair. As I looked at my reflection in the mirror, I wondered how wrinkles could seemingly appear overnight! My mother always says she's shocked when she looks in the mirror and doesn't see a twenty-five-year-old looking back. I agree!!! Although I don't think I would ever do anything surgically, I do like my lotions and potions. That being said, I opened the facial masks sheet that guaranteed it would give me tighter and brighter skin and covered my face. "Relax, and kick back while the all-natural ingredients in this super hydrating mask floods your skin with intense weightless hydration. In just fifteen minutes you will have rehydrated and radiant skin." Laying on the bed waiting for the mask to work its magic, I heard Peter walk into the room. He didn't say a word. He didn't need to. One of three boys, he's never understood the female need to primp.

Chapter 2

The house filled with friends and comfortable chatter as conversation varied from holiday travel and New Year's resolutions to the latest research grant secured by DFU's prestigious J.R. Whiteley Research Center. The neighborhood residents' careers varied, but the majority were related to the university. Phillip and Ann Andrews were the exception to the rule. An attorney and drama teacher, they were questioning the university's president, Randall Weber, about the significance of the grant.

"The Defense Advanced Research Projects Agency, also known as DARPA, is an agency of the Defense Department. Grants provide funding to create centers that help develop emerging technologies for use by the military," shared Randall. "In our case, we will be working on systems to detect and evaluate bacterial pathogens."

"This sounds like a big dang deal," commented Ann. As Phillip and a few other neighbors continued to question Randall about the grant, I could see Ann's eyes were beginning to glaze over. Having been raised in a career military family, I knew the signs of information overkill. Channeling my mother's deftness at rescuing guests from such a conversation, I extracted Ann from the group and directed her towards a more compatible conversation.

Circulating through the clusters of friends, neighbors and colleagues that seemed to fill every corner of my home, I found Lane in our study with Kevin Crank looking at the map of the world that dominated the west wall. Because of Peter's position as director of the Hanser Center for Global Education and my childhood as an Air Force brat, we've traveled extensively throughout Europe, Russia and Turkey. Early in our marriage we started 'pinning' places we visited on a map. When we settled in our house on Creekside Drive, we created a permanent "Wall of the World". One of our family traditions was to pin holiday cards we received from friends onto the map marking their location.

"Lane was just explaining the map's significance to me. You certainly have a lot of international friends. It's very impressive," said Kevin.

"We've been blessed over the years. You'll notice we don't have many cards from Asia so there's definitely room to expand our friend base," I quipped.

"Technically, the majority of Russia is on the Asian continent, so I'd say you have a toehold there," Kevin pointed out. "In fact, I recognize the name on one of the cards, Dmitry Sergey. Isn't he a pretty influential international businessman?"

"He has done very well for himself although, our connection with him goes back to when he and Peter were foreign exchange students in Germany. The two of them became quick friends and have stayed in touch for all of these years."

"We actually met up with him and his family in Croatia about ten years ago," chimed in Lane.

"Always good to have friends in high places," remarked Kevin.

"Lane, is this your new beau?" The question came from Miss Essie, the neighborhood's longest resident. Still living in the house where she was born, she would celebrate her 80th birthday this year. Miss Essie was known for her unique sense of style, collection of tennis shoes for any occasion and memorable expressions. Tonight, she sported a red, sequined beanie, light up holiday sweater and candy-cane covered sneakers. Her earrings looked as if they had been fashioned out of tinsel covered pipe cleaners.

"No, ma'am. This is Kevin Crank. He's the one remodeling the house down the street," Lane quickly explained.

Peering through glasses that covered nearly half her face, Miss Essie proclaimed, "Sometimes love straddles you on the nose and pokes you in the eye." With that, she turned and moved on.

Kevin awkwardly looked at his shoes as Lane and I shared a knowing smile. Neighborhood residents learned a long time ago to roll with Miss Essie's adages. Fortunately, Jake and Diane Thorne, as well as Lane's friend, Sara, joined us. The conversation turned to life in Deep Fork and away from potential romance.

I moved on mingling with our other guests, refilling trays of food and making sure drinks were replenished. As was usual in any neighborhood gathering, 'the general' had cornered a few people who had not maintained their yards to his standards. Fondly nicknamed 'the general' by anyone who had spent time with him, Bill Walker and his wife, Jo, had lived in the neighborhood nearly fifty years. Tonight, his focus was on Gary Barrett and Sofia Gomez. Gary joined the Whiteley Research Center as director three years ago. Sofia worked with Peter in the Hanser Center for Global Education. Overhearing the words lawn service and nut grass, I knew 'the general' was on a mission and had his targets in his sights. I signaled to Peter to intervene, hoping to give Gary and Sofia a chance to make their escape.

Around 10:00 p.m. guests began to gather their coats and say their good-byes. Randall and his wife, Jean, stayed after everyone else departed to help us clean. Peter and I often discussed how rare it was to find a couple with which we equally clicked. Within months of the Webers taking up residency across the street, we'd become friends. Over the years, we've played hours of cards, shared the joys and tribulations of parenting, discussed university and world politics and even traveled together.

While Peter and Randall finished taking out trash and recycling, Jean, Lane and I sat down for a little post party talk.

"I noticed 'the general' was making the rounds tonight," Lane commented. "Sounds like he's still patrolling the neighborhood looking for infractions."

Jean giggled as she recanted his inspection of Kevin Crank's renovation project. "Millie and I were walking along the creek path. The two of them were standing in the back yard, arms akimbo. Even from a distance I could tell Kevin was getting an earful of advice on what he was or wasn't doing. Honestly, I think we are all just grateful something is happening with that eyesore."

"So, what's his story?" queried Lane.

"As I understand it, he went through a rather difficult divorce," offered Jean. "From what I've deduced he needed a change of scenery."

"Well Deep Fork's definitely not the obvious choice for someone his age," pointed out Lane. "I mean it was a great place to grow up but not so much for a single guy."

I added to the story with information I'd gleaned over the three months since he moved here. "Well, there is more to the story. I think you knew the house was originally owned by his great, great uncle and aunt. After his divorce he bought the house from other family members, moved here and took a job at DFU in the IT department. He also runs an IT consulting business from his home. A little stand offish but seems nice enough."

"I think he's cute, what do you think, Lane?" Jean teased. As the two of them bantered back and forth, I kept quiet. I refuse to even give a glimmer of my opinion when it came to my daughter's love life. However, if she asked, which I doubt she will, I'd warn her to stay away from Kevin. He seems to have a lot of baggage and I really don't want my daughter's tender heart broken again. During college, she dated a nice enough guy and I suppose we all thought they would get married. However, after graduation they moved to different cities and eventually broke up. Although she downplayed the break up, I could see the hurt in her eyes. That was three years ago and she still hasn't dated anyone seriously.

About that time, Peter and Randall joined us with an open bottle of wine and five glasses. Lane begged off since she had to leave early the next morning and still needed to pack (my guess is she knew the conversation would move to university gossip). The four of us settled in front of the fire and sipped our wine.

"So Whiteley Research Center hooked another big one, being named a DARPA Center," Peter led with. "Indeed, they did," Randall confirmed. "It really is an honor for the university. Victor was quite instrumental in enabling us to land this one." Victor Anderson is the Vice President of Research at DFU. In the twelve years he's been at the university he's risen through the ranks first as department head of biochemistry, then associate dean of research until he took over the vice presidency three years ago.

"Victor, as well as his team at the research center, have spent the last couple years recruiting and putting together some top scientists, with this prize in mind. It really is a win, win for all of us. Speaking of landing a big fish, when do you leave for the Global Education Symposium?" Randall asked Peter. "I head for Barcelona the 15th of January. It really is an honor to be asked to participate on the panel. If David Hanser was still with us, I'm sure he'd be both amazed and thrilled to see where his vision has taken the center and the university. The fact that seventy percent of our students have some type of international experience is impressive."

As the two of them continued their talk concerning university politics, Jean and I turned our conversation to the spring semester and what was left to do to prepare for our classes. Jean teaches in the psychology department and I'm an adjunct instructor in the English department. During the fall semester, my primary role is advising students. Except for the few totally oblivious students or parents trying to micro-manage their child's life, I really love getting to know the students and helping them navigate their way through the college experience.

However, the spring semester is my favorite! This is when I get to teach my "signature" class, Exploring Race Through Literature. Using four books, I lead students through an exploration of racial experiences in our country. Two books (based on factual events) take place in Oklahoma, *Fire in Beulah* and *Killers of the Flower Moon*. It is always a sobering experience for students to realize the atrocities that took place not so long ago in our own backyard. The other two books, *Black Like Me* and *To Kill a Mockingbird*, are really about perspective. In the words of Scout, *"You never really know a man until you stand in his shoes and walk around in them."* My hope in this class is to help my students see the world through different eyes, and hopefully become better people as a result. A noble undertaking. It's one of the reasons I value Peter's position so much.

The Hanser Center for Global Education was founded in 1970 through an endowment by former petroleum engineering graduate and philanthropist, David Hanser. The mission of the center is to broaden the world view of students by introducing them to architecture throughout the world and its context within culture, history and politics. When Peter was recruited for the position, he was leery, fearing it would take him away from his first passion - architectural history. However, the opposite happened. It's allowed him to travel more extensively than he ever dreamed, share his passion for architecture and create a bridge for launching students into a global market. As important as the education students receive in the classroom is, many report their international travel is what changed their world.

As we drained the last of the wine from the bottle and watched the embers die in the fire, the Webers said their goodbyes and walked across the street to their house. The 'President's Mansion' as it is known in our community, is one of the largest homes in the neighborhood and was built in the Federalist style. Boasting an expansive front lawn, the rear of the house overlooks a creek which divides our neighborhood from Deep Fork University. Looking up at the starlit sky, I found myself for the second time that day thankful for my home and neighborhood.

I took the wine glasses to the kitchen and rinsed them out before turning in. As I started my nighttime routine and prepared to slather anti-aging cream over my face, Peter stepped behind me and put his arms around my waist. Although there is not much difference in our height, that is where our similarities end. He has wonderful thick, wavy dark hair which is just starting to gray. I have straight as an arrow blonde hair (that will never gray if I have anything to say about it).

"You throw a good party, Ev," he said as he gave me a hug. Looking at the two of us in the mirror, a warmth encompassed me as I once again gave thanks for my husband. I turned to face him as he took my face in his hands and kissed me tenderly, "I love you." Three simple words but oh so powerful.

Chapter 3

"Be sure to text us when you get home," I reminded Lane as she threw her computer bag into the backseat. Although I am not a fatalist, I am a worrier. Not so much about the little things, but about the safety and well-being of those I love. I think anyone who has lost someone close to them harbors those fears. Especially if it was a child.

Bobby was only three years old when he was diagnosed with leukemia. The next year was filled with hospital stays, chemotherapy, periods of hope and in the end, the ultimate devastation. Lane was six when Bobby died. I've heard children often times feel it's their fault when someone close to them dies. Children aren't the only ones who carry that guilt. The "what if's" nearly drove Peter and me apart as we processed grief in our own ways. In many ways, Lane became the caregiver during that period. I suppose there are times she still plays that role. Peter and I knew that if we were going to survive, we had to make a change. We moved to Deep Fork a year after Bobby died. Some might call it fate that the opening at the Hanser Global Education center coincided with this time in our lives. I prefer to think it was divine intervention. My parents had recently retired to Oklahoma City after dad's last tour of duty at Tinker Air Force Base. Being near family, in a new environment, meeting new professional challenges, gave us the fresh start we needed.

The feelings of fear, sadness and loss that had been a part of me since Bobby's death, washed over me as we waved goodbye to

The Neighborhood

Lane. Just then 'the general' approached us on his morning tour of the neighborhood. "I see Lane is headed back to Dallas," he said crisply. "Now that your party is over, I assume your holiday decorations will be coming down as well. I've checked the weather forecast, mid-50's, no wind and sunny all day." Always on patrol, he made sure (with the exception of an ice storm) everyone had the neighborhood back to pre-holiday order by January 7th. "I noticed the Marshall family has not properly prepared their tree for curbside pick-up. One of the boys' probably drug it to the curb. I'll let Alan and Tracey know what they need to do." And he was off.

"I guess I've been given my orders for the day," smiled Peter. "I'll take the inside if you'll take the outside," I offered. Pounding footsteps made both of us turn as Kevin ran by. His quick wave certainly did not meet the 'good neighbor' standards of the neighborhood. "He's an interesting fellow," reflected Peter. "Did I tell you he was quizzing me about Dmitry last night?"

"He and Lane were looking at the map of the world and he honed in on Dmitry's holiday card. Apparently, he knew of Dmitry's reputation in the international market," I offered.

"Hmmm," was the only response I got as his gaze followed Kevin. My husband can be a man of few words. A deep thinker but not a talker.

With all of the holiday trappings packed up and put away for another year, we collapsed in front of the television and enjoyed leftovers from the previous night's party. "Are you up for an astronomy outing tonight?" questioned Peter. "The sky's clear, there's a full moon and it isn't freezing outside. I could pack up my telescope and we could head out to the Wildlife Refuge."

It takes a lot for me to get out once I've sunk into the couch, but I am a sucker for a beautiful night sky! I offered to make the hot chocolate as he gathered the telescope, camping chairs and a few blankets. Darkness enveloped us as we left Deep Fork and drove towards the refuge. The fifteen-minute drive was filled with the mellow voice of James Taylor reminding us to enjoy the passage of time.

Peter turned and winked at me, "No one I'd rather spend my life with, Ev." I countered his wink with a smile and an "I love you." Several years ago, we had attended a relationship building workshop through our church. One of the exercises was to list three traits you admire about your spouse. The traits I focused on for Peter were principled, trustworthy and curious. When I say curious, I don't mean nosy. He just has a deep interest in learning about almost anything. Since the day I met him he has generally had one or two books he is reading simultaneously. Once the internet became so accessible there has been no stopping his bent to acquire information. As far as being principled and trustworthy, I know deep in my soul that I can trust Peter. He is my rock.

The traits Peter chose to describe me were a kind heart, creative and loyal. When Peter says creative, he was not referring to any artistic propensity. It was a positive way of saying, I rarely will take no for an answer. I firmly believe there has to be a way to solve any problem, everything is figureoutable. A trait he admires, but occasionally, I suspect, drives him a little crazy. I actually wrote out each of our lists and taped them to the inside of our bathroom's medicine cabinet. Over the years, when things have been tense between us, we've both referred back to the list. It helps to keep us focused on what we value and admire about each other.

The stars were absolutely mesmerizing from our vantage point at the top of the hill. As we sat huddled under blankets enjoying our hot chocolate, Peter would occasionally look through the telescope and remark on a constellation. I, on the other hand, preferred just sitting and enjoying the beauty of the night sky. Although Oklahoma was not known for its dramatic landscape, it does offer unrivaled beauty in the sky. Whether it is the flashing of lightning

The Neighborhood

across the sky, a sunset with brilliant hues of oranges and pinks or the heavens bursting with stars, for me it is awe inspiring.

As we approached town, Peter mentioned he needed to stop by his office to pick up some reading in preparation for the conference in Barcelona. We skirted downtown via College Street and turned into the main entrance of DFU just past the edge of downtown. On our left was the plaza that helped define the entry to campus. Although the fountains were turned off during the winter months, the illuminated library lay motionless in the reflecting pool. On our right was the Hanser Center for Global Education.

Housed in one of the original campus buildings, the Hanser Center was built in the craftsman style. The portico created a welcoming entrance. At one point, almost every DFU student crosses the threshold looking for their chance to see the world. Peter's office is on the first floor with a great view of the reflecting pool and fountains. I stayed in the car as Peter ran in to get his materials. As I continued to enjoy James Taylor and the car's seat warmers, I caught sight of some movement ahead of me. Turning the corner between the Whiteley Research Center and the Health Sciences building, I spied the tall lanky figure of Kevin Crank, once again running. I've always been suspicious of people who exercise too much, especially runners. It seems to me; they are running away from something.

I was debating whether or not to roll down the window and make some clever quip when Peter came out. He reached the sidewalk just as Kevin was about to cross. Both men were clearly in their own worlds as they looked up just in time to avoid a collision. Acknowledging each other with a nod, Kevin continued his run and Peter got in the car.

"Can we make one more stop before we head home? I need to pick up a few things at the Corner Market," I asked.

We parked the car and went into the small but well stocked store. You might not be able to get everything you wanted at the Corner Market, but you could certainly get everything you needed. We grabbed a basket and began to pick up a few staples. As we were in the process of picking out the perfect bananas (not too ripe, not too green), we heard the familiar voices of our neighbors Manasi & Kamya Patel. Originally from India, they had come to the United States via England where Manasi had studied medicine. A few years older than Peter and me, they had moved to Deep Fork shortly after we did. A leader in the field of vaccine enhancement, it had been a real coup when DFU recruited him to not only teach in the Health Sciences school but also to join the Whiteley Research Center. His expertise and reputation undoubtedly were instrumental in the center receiving the DARPA grant. Kamya shared her time and talents as a volunteer in the city's Free Health Clinic, the English as a Second Language Center and regularly went on mission trips associated with global vaccination.

"I didn't realize you were home. How was your visit with Tapa?" I asked. "It was quite good," Kamya answered. Although she had left India while in her mid-20's, she still spoke with the beautiful nearly lyrical cadence of her native land. "Jaan surprised us by coming from Seattle. It was delightful to have our whole family together. But Chicago is very cold this time of year, so we are pleased to be home." After a few more pleasantries, we went our separate ways, paid for our groceries and headed home.

The next morning, I was wheeling the garbage can in from the curb when I heard Jean shouting my name. "Did you hear about the excitement at the research lab last night? There was a break in! The police called Randall about 9:00 pm, Min was there catching up on some work and she was attacked! Someone came up from behind and knocked her out!"

"What? Is she okay?"

"Yes, Randall was at the hospital till about 2:00 a.m. while they checked her out. She's resting at home with what I'm going to guess is a pretty good knot on the back of her head. Needless to say, she was pretty shaken up." While Jean caught her breath, I tried to process what had happened. Things like this just did not happen in Deep Fork.

"I was going to make some chicken noodle soup today so I'll take some over for Min and the family." I was already moving into helpful neighbor mode. "Any idea why someone broke into the center?"

"Victor and Gary met the police and did a walk through. Nothing seemed out of order but they'll need to do a sweep of all the computers to see if they were tampered with. Randall said Kevin Crank has a special certification in computer forensics which will help them detect if anything was compromised."

Later as I was chopping vegetables and adding them to the simmering broth, I couldn't squelch the uneasy feeling that was beginning to grow in the pit of my stomach. Ours was a quiet town, where you smile and wave at someone even if you don't know them. A safe place where you don't have to worry about getting knocked over the head. Feeling my little corner of the world had been violated, I could only imagine what Min was feeling. I packed up the soup and added a fresh batch of chocolate chip cookies, knowing Min's sons would appreciate them more than the soup.

I cut through our back yard and made a slight jog to the left as I came alongside the Jungs' house. Cynthia was just walking down the front steps as I turned the corner. "Obviously you heard about Min, the poor dear" she said. "Such a disturbing episode for such a sweet family."

"Jean told me about it this morning. It's just awful! She said Victor walked through the center with the police."

"Yes, he didn't get home till well after midnight. Hopefully, they'll be able to do a more thorough investigation today." We visited a few more minutes before Cynthia headed next door to her house. I often marveled at what a good listener Cynthia was. Unlike most people, she rarely made the conversation about herself. She always expressed interest in what you were doing, where you went and what you thought on almost any subject. I made a mental note to add 'be a better listener' to my growing list of New Year's resolutions.

As I walked up the front steps of the Jung's' home, I recalled the first time I met them. Jin was directing movers while Min was trying to keep the boys out of harm's way. Sam was just learning to walk and Mee, as any three-year-old would, was totally mesmerized by the large moving truck. They were coming from North Carolina where Jin had worked at a molecular biology center. Come to think of it, I had brought them chocolate chip cookies that day as well.

Jin answered the door and expressed gratitude for the soup and cookies. Knowing Cynthia had just left, I chose to make my visit brief. I offered for the boys to come over after school so Min could continue to rest. Jin appreciatively acknowledged the invitation but shared arrangements had already been made for the Andrew boys to pick Sam and Mee up from school. A few years their senior, Steve and Doug Andrew were definitely their preferred babysitters. As was par for the course, the neighborhood was willing and ready to lend a hand.

Chapter 4

The sunshine we'd enjoyed for the last few days disappeared as clouds moved in and a greyness enveloped us as the temperature dropped. Still, a week away from the start of the spring semester, our plan was to work from home whilst we enjoyed a roaring fire. Peter was firing up his computer while I finished cleaning up from breakfast. I heard him swear under his breath as he tried to log on to the internet.

"I don't know what is going on with this blasted internet. This is the third day in a row I've had to go through the process of reconnecting. I had the same problem when I was streaming a movie last night."

"I can call our provider's help line and see if they can walk me through a solution," I offered. We both hated dealing with computer issues and were more likely to go to a coffee shop or the office than deal with technical issues. Today was no different. Peter packed up his bag and headed towards his office. I was relegated the task of calling tech support.

After being on hold for thirty minutes and going through the process of unhooking everything, counting to ten and reattaching all of the wires, it seemed to be working. I called Peter and let him know we were back on-line, but he was already absorbed in his preparation for the Barcelona trip so I found myself home alone.

A few New Year gifts were still taking up shelf space waiting to be delivered to neighbors. I quickly calculated who might be home on a weekday morning and filled my basket with the jars containing dry ingredients for soup. Over the years, I've found people are inundated with treats throughout December. Receiving fixings for a hearty soup in January always seems to be appreciated. I also think it is a little more sensitive to our international neighbors whose faith does not include the celebration of Christmas. In the end, I will have delivered around fifteen jars throughout the neighborhood. But today, I only had three to hand out.

My first stop was at the Thomas household. Arnold was a retired insurance agent and Lynda was still actively selling real estate. She had cornered the market in finding homes for incoming university faculty. I knew my morning would be lost if I didn't play my cards right. As much as I liked Arnold, he was a talker. My mom has an expression, "Ask him the time and he'll tell you how to build a watch." That definitely summed up Arnold! I strategized a maximum of twenty minutes for chitchat and set my phone to vibrate at the designated time. After hearing, in detail, about Arnold's on-going battle with moles, the vibrating phone let me know it was time to extricate myself. Pointing at the other jars in my basket, I wished him well with his mole war, excused myself and moved on to the Patel's house.

As always, Kamya was extremely gracious and invited me in for one of her specialty herbal teas and a biscuit. As a little girl, Lane had been quite perplexed about the disparity between my biscuits and Kamya's. It took me several months to realize Kamya was using the British term for cookies. Lane and I still smile knowingly at each other when offered a biscuit.

I always have a sense of being transported when I enter the Patel's house. The faint scent of exotic spices hangs lightly in the air and music native to India often plays soothingly in the background. No matter the season, Kamya always seems to have just brewed a tea to complement the weather and baked some type of delicacy. An hour spent in this environment always infuses me with a sense of serenity.

My final stop was Kevin Crank's house. Crossing the street, I once again found myself wondering about his story. I still find it difficult to comprehend this new generation who works from home. I understand computers and the internet have in many cases made the need to show up at an office obsolete, but I wonder if that's healthy. Wouldn't you miss the social interaction? Maybe that is why Kevin is always running…. trying to find someone to talk to. As Lane would say, "It's really none of your business, mom."

After two rings, I was about to leave when Kevin finally answered the door. I wished him a Happy New Year and offered him the jar of soup. The protocol in the neighborhood is *always* to invite someone in when they come to your door. You don't have to accept, but the invitation should be offered. Apparently, Kevin had not received the 'memo'. He quickly thanked me and moved as if to shut the door. I do not consider myself pushy or even overly assertive, but I did think it was time Kevin began to understand what it means to be neighborly. I made a swift move to at least get partially past the front door and asked, "How are your home renovations coming along?" Obviously, an opportunity for him to show me his work.

"I've been busy with work so they've slowed. I'll get on it in a few weeks, if weather permits," he hesitatingly offered.

"We're all excited to see the work you've done." Certainly, this was an opportunity for him to give me a tour of work done so far. He didn't bite.

"When I'm finished, I'll have people over." Having gone through a major remodel project about ten years ago, I knew you were never really done. However, I can take a hint and began to turn to leave when I spotted the camera on his table. I don't know much about photography but recognized the long-range lens attached to the camera. My dad has a similar one for his bird watching expeditions.

"Are you an aspiring ornithologist?"

"Excuse me," Kevin asked in a confused tone.

"The camera and long-range lens. My dad has a similar set up for bird watching."

"Oh yes, I've really just begun."

Okay, so that conversation hit a dead end. I may not be the sharpest pencil in the box, but I know when it's time to leave. I wished him luck on his remodeling project and headed back to my house.

Once home, I lit a fire, settled into the couch, covered my legs with a throw and picked up my well-worn copy of *To Kill a Mockingbird* in preparation for my spring class. I don't feel the need to re-read every book I use in my course each semester, but I at least revisit them every few years. This American classic has been one of my favorite books since first reading it in high school. A perfect read on a gray January day.

The next day, Peter and I were in the midst of our morning routine when we heard the sirens. Stepping onto the front porch, we could see an ambulance as well as several patrol cars parked across the street in Randall and Jean's driveway. I instinctively grabbed Peter's arm as fear washed over me. Although Randall took good care of himself, he was a 60-year-old man with a family history of heart issues. Poor Jean. Just as my heart was sinking, I sighted our dear friends come around the side of their house deep in discussion with a police officer. Knowing something serious must have happened, I still couldn't help but give a prayer of thanksgiving that our friends were safe.

Instinctively, I wanted to run over, but Peter pulled me back and said, "Wait." We grabbed a couple of blankets and sat on our porch swing whilst we waited. It seemed like an eternity, but Jean finally made her way to our porch. She was white as a sheet and visibly shaken. Clenching tightly to her Golden Retriever's leash, she tearfully shared, "It's 'the general'. He's dead. Millie and I were walking the trail along the creek and found his body. He must have fallen and hit his head on a rock."

"Poor Jo," I murmured as tears filled my eyes. The three of us stood in silence as the graveness of the news settled in. "Jo is visiting their daughters in Oklahoma City. I have their younger daughter's phone number. Should I call her? I'd rather they hear the news from friends than the police." When Bobby died, Peter had made all the calls. I could not bring myself to say the words, "He's gone." Two decades later, the pain seemed just as fresh. Losing someone is never easy. True, 'the general' had lived a long, good life. But he was still loved and would be dearly missed, especially by Jo. Just last summer they had celebrated their 60th anniversary.

Jean received permission from the police officers to notify Jo and we went inside to make the call. By then, the street was filling with neighbors anxious to hear what had happened. Peter worked his way through the gathering crowd sharing what information he had. Before making the call, I brewed some tea, buying a bit of time before I delivered the heartbreaking news. As the water began to boil, I contemplated how one phone call can change the course of a life.

Jean mindlessly stroked Millie's neck as she sipped her tea. My fingers shook as I found the number for 'the general' and Jo's daughter, Vicky. There is never an easy way to share this type of news. My conversation with Vicky was relatively short considering the severity of the news. I ended the call and looked at Jean who was staring out the front window. "I can't seem to get warm," she spoke quietly as she took another sip of tea. "I keep thinking of him lying there helpless in the cold, hurt and afraid." I hugged her closely as we both let tears fall gently down our faces.

Chapter 5

A few days later neighbors, friends and family gathered at First Baptist church for 'the general's' funeral. As is the case in many towns developed in the 1920's and 30's, churches were an inherent part of the downtown's fabric. Known as the "Four Corners", the Methodist, Catholic, Presbyterian and Baptist churches stood sentry like watch towers in a walled city. Bill and Jo had been members of First Baptist for more than 50 years. They had seen their daughters baptized and married in this church, spent countless hours serving on committees, taught Sunday School and worshiped in the sanctuary. And today, we were here to say our goodbyes and honor Bill's life.

Jo, her two daughters and their families had arrived later the same day as 'the general's' body had been found. Since then it had been a steady stream of friends and neighbors stopping by to share their condolences and bring a covered dish. After today, things would begin to return to 'normal'. Whatever that means when you lose a loved one.

Lane came home for the service. In many ways, the Walkers had been surrogate grandparents for our daughter. Lane was only six when we moved in next door to Bill and Jo. They had periodically babysat, brought her trinkets, attended dance recitals and always took an interest in what she was doing, where she was going and if she was dating anyone.

Lane sat between Peter and me during the service. The three of us held hands as stories, scriptures and songs were shared. We started this tradition at Bobby's funeral. Although the grief of losing my precious boy is not as suffocating as it once was, it still sneaks up at unexpected times. For me, that was rarely at a funeral. To this day a smell, sound or image will trigger a memory and my heart will begin to ache. Just a few months ago, a ball from the Jung boys ended up in our back yard. Looking out my kitchen window, the sight of the ball sparked a memory of Bobby and Lane kicking a ball back and forth. As a tear welled up in my eye, I squeezed Lane's hand. Today's service celebrated a life well lived. The real grieving would come in the days, weeks and months ahead.

After the service, we all gathered in the church basement for cookies, punch and another chance to share stories and murmur our disbelief at 'the general's' passing. Peter had walked over to visit with Victor and Cynthia. Lane made the circuit of neighbors while I headed in the opposite direction to say hello to the Bensons. Matthew and Lauren have two little girls, Emma and Hannah. Since they had moved here from New Jersey, Peter and I (following the example of the Walkers) have taken on the role of surrogate grandparents for the two girls. When I'm having a bad day, I can count on a dose of cuteness from those two little munchkins. Today, I needed a larger dose than normal.

Matthew excused himself, leaving Lauren and me to visit. "As tragic as it is, somehow it seems fitting 'the general' would die while on patrol," I reflected as I munched on a cookie.

"That's just it, Evelyn. Something about this accident just doesn't feel right to me. Did I ever tell you I was a nurse at a trauma center back in New Jersey? We were sorely understaffed, so I ended up serving many roles including helping the coroner. Over the three years I worked there, I saw a lot of head traumas. When they brought 'the general's' body to the hospital, I offered to escort it to the morgue. It just seemed like the right thing to do. Anyway, I was on duty when the coroner checked his body. I know he ruled it an accident, but there seem to be discrepancies between where the trauma to the head was and how he would have had to fall for that type of injury," Lauren told me in a quiet voice.

"What are you saying? That it wasn't an accident?" I asked,

shocked at the thought that it could be anything sinister.

"It's just a gut feeling, and obviously the police see it as an accident. But, if their timeline is correct, he would have had to have been walking along the creek path close to sundown. Does that sound like 'the general'? I mean, he might have been inspecting my mulch or checking to see if your address could be seen from the street, but I never recall him going down to the creek that time of day."

"I'm really not sure how to process all of this," I shuddered. "Shouldn't the police be following up on this information?"

"I've noted all my concerns with the officer in charge of the investigation as well as our county coroner. Neither seems to take much stock in what I had to say. They just assume he was an old man who got addled, wandered off and unfortunately fell. As plausible as that scenario may sound, it just doesn't ring true for 'the general'."

"What does Matthew think?" I queried.

"I haven't said anything to him. He's so absorbed and uptight about his department's upcoming audit, I didn't want to add my speculation to his stress level. I mean, it's just a gut feeling and I certainly don't want to start any rumors that would get back to Jo."

"I agree. You've done what you need to by sharing your insights with the police. I suppose it is in their court to pursue any type of investigation," I doubtfully said.

"Please don't mention this to anyone, except maybe Peter," Lauren whispered under her breath as Peter, Victor and Cynthia joined us.

"This is all so tragic, not only for Jo. I feel sorry for Jean finding the body. We had a long talk yesterday over a cup of tea. She is still pretty shaken up over the ordeal," Cynthia shared.

"It was definitely upsetting for her," Peter murmured.

"Lauren, I understand you were at the hospital when 'the general's' body arrived," Victor abruptly interjected. "I imagine it's tough to see someone you know come through the doors, especially in a case like this."

Almost under her breath Lauren said, "Always."

Other neighbors began to join us, including Miss Essie. Never one to conform to societal standards, today she wore a black cape covered with colorful pom poms, rivaled only by her light-up tennis shoes. Conversation naturally turned to the unfortunate circumstances surrounding 'the general's' death and memories of his neighborhood patrols.

"I'm going to miss 'the general's' inspection of my hydrangeas. His keen eye always helped me keep them in top shape," Cynthia shared as she dabbed at her eyes.

"Life is a game played with marked cards," Miss Essie reflected. "Looks like it was time for Bill to cash in his chips." As was often the case after one of her insightful comments, everyone seemed at a loss for words. Finally, someone mentioned the weather and conversation resumed.

As the crowd began to disburse, Peter, Lane and I said our good-byes to Jo and her daughters and headed home. It was a quiet ride home as we were each lost in our thoughts. I kept playing the conversation I had with Lauren over and over in my head. Could 'the general's' death be anything but an accident?

Peter was scheduled to leave the next day for his conference in Barcelona. Although he is very meticulous in his preparation and planning, there were still a lot of last-minute e-mails waiting to be answered, packing to do and confirming of travel arrangements. In other words, he was very pre-occupied.

That left Lane and me to re-hash who we had seen at the funeral, what was said and share any gossip we might have picked up. This would have driven Peter crazy. I've learned over the years, the influence of a devout Catholic mother and the stoic Scandinavian ancestry my Minnesotan born husband boasts does not lead to idle conversation, especially gossip. I built a fire, brewed a pot of tea and the two of us nestled into overstuffed couches. Lane covered herself with a throw as I stretched my legs onto the ottoman.

"Min told me about the attack last week at the Whiteley Center. That is so crazy! She still seemed pretty shaken up. What do you think they were after?"

"That seems to be the million-dollar question. They do some pretty high-level research and now that they have the DARPA contract, that should intensify. But as far as anyone can tell, nothing was taken or tampered with. Kevin Crank, the man you met at our holiday party, has a certification in computer forensics, so he is going through all of the computers to look for any abnormalities."

"Holy Buckets!" Peter exclaimed as he marched out of his office. "The internet is down again!"

"Are you still having problems with that?" Lane inquired.

"Yes, it seems to be solved by unplugging everything, waiting ten minutes and then re-hooking the wires. But it is definitely getting old. I'm going to call tomorrow and see if I can get a physical body to come and look at our system," I shared with more than a little exasperation in my voice.

Lane went to finish preparing for her return trip to Dallas, Peter moved to the bedroom to do his own packing and I went into our shared office space to do my re-boot tango. As I waited the specified ten minutes before I re-attached wires, I pondered what Lauren had said. Could 'the general's' death be anything but an accident? If it wasn't an accident, who would have done such a thing? Was it a random act of violence or had he been targeted? I made a mental note to make sure all the doors were locked, especially with Peter leaving for a week. I had always felt safe in our neighborhood and was pretty lax about securing the house when I would leave, or at night. But now, the knot in my stomach told me it would be wise to err on the side of caution until some of my questions were answered.

As Peter and I cuddled in bed that night, I shared with him Lauren's comments concerning 'the general's' death. He was quiet for a long time before he almost inaudibly said "That's disturbing." I was really hoping he would dismiss the notion; tell me everything was okay and we would both fall asleep reassured life was normal. "Lauren has a good head on her shoulders," Peter reflected. "I don't think of her as prone to creating scenarios like this." Neither of us had much to say after that, but each of us lay awake for quite a while lost in our own thoughts.

The next morning, both of my travelers packed their cars. Lane headed south to Dallas and Peter headed north to the Tulsa airport. I went inside to call our internet provider, determined to have an actual person deal with our on-going problem. I scheduled someone for the next morning, packed my oversized purse and headed to campus to prepare for the beginning of the spring semester. I had almost pulled my car out of the garage when I remembered my vow to make sure all doors were locked. After 'securing the premises', I headed to work.

Chapter 6

Reviewing my notes from *Killers of the Flower Moon*, I again pondered how people could treat each other with such a lack of humanity. The other component of the story that is especially haunting for me is the lack of voice for those who were victimized. My thoughts immediately turned to 'the general'. Was he a victim of a crime? Who would hear his cry for justice?

I was haunted with these thoughts as I pulled my car into the garage. Seeing the lights on next door, I decided to check in on Jo before settling in for the evening. The Walkers' oldest daughter, Betty, opened the door. We exchanged a hug and briefly discussed how Jo was dealing with everything. As Betty led me into the living room, I was keenly aware of the stillness that filled the house. At least for now, time seemed to have stood still as Jo and her daughters absorbed the paradigm shift their lives had taken.

Jo had always been small in stature, but now seemed almost swallowed by the stack of cards neatly stacked next to her favorite rocking chair. Looking up as we entered the living room, she graced me with her sweet smile and invited me to sit down. Obviously, she was slowly and methodically going through each card, treasuring the kind words of sympathy.

Betty excused herself to the kitchen to join her sister, Vicky, in once again reorganizing the refrigerator to accommodate all the food brought by friends and family.

"Thank you so much for stopping in, dear. You and Peter have

The Neighborhood

always been so sweet to Bill and me," Jo said as she absent-mindedly adjusted the blanket thrown over her shoulders. "People are being so kind to me." Although she seemed quite composed, I could see the deep well of sadness in her eyes. "I've heard from so many dear friends Bill and I knew over the years.

A few years after Bobby died, I attended a training on how to minister to people going through loss. One of the skills, which resonated with me, was the power of listening and of being silent. Jo just needed someone to listen to her, not give platitudes or share their own stories of loss. Just listen. That's what I did. For the next hour, Jo went through every card she'd received and shared stories of their connection with the people who sent them. At times, she would tear up and other times would smile. All part of a process I knew only too well.

"I also got a call from Eleanor Crank. Her husband was the nephew of the couple who built the ugly house down the street. You know the one that nice young man is fixing up. When Eleanor and her husband would come to visit, we would always get together. Our kids were the same ages so we would meet in the park. While the children played, we visited. That house was not built for children so she appreciated having a friend in the neighborhood. I hadn't heard from her in years, but she saw mention of Bill's passing on a veterans' website. You know, at our age, you check the obituaries. Anyway, she called to express her sympathy and we must have visited for 30 minutes."

"Hearing from friends has always been a comfort to me," I shared.

"Oh yes, dear. But like most of us, she is beginning to have memory issues. I know the signs only too well. I mentioned her grandson remodeling the house, and I could tell she was confused. Did not even remember he had moved here. It just gets harder and harder to keep everything straight...." she reflected as her voice trailed off.

Just then Vicky came in with a tray of food for her mom. Although she offered to make one for me as well, I declined, gave Jo a hug, said my good-byes and headed home.

As I heated up leftovers from the previous night's dinner, my thoughts began to wander. When I say wander, I mean really wander. They jumped from class preparations, to Jean's ashen face as she told us about finding 'the general' to Kevin Crank always running, to reminding myself to refill the prescriptions lined up on the bathroom counter. If Jo says it gets harder and harder to keep everything straight as we get older, I am in DEEP trouble.

That's where my thoughts finally settled. How sad that Kevin's grandmother could not even remember he had bought the house and moved to Deep Fork. Would the day come that I would not be able to recall the name of my loved ones? Okay, in the words of Peter, "Ev, there is no need to borrow trouble."

I spent the rest of the evening on class preparations, re-reading my notes from previous lectures and highlighting issues I wanted to emphasize with the students. Before heading to bed, I double checked to make sure all doors were locked and once again opened my e-mail hoping to have a confirmation from Peter that he had arrived safely. I'm use to Peter travelling and have willed myself not to obsess and worry, but I always feel better when I know he is safe. Once communicating internationally became much easier, I invoked the daily e-mail rule. He doesn't have to say much. Just a note to say he's arrived, doing fine and he gets 'extra points' if he says he misses me. Peter earns a lot of extra points. The e-mail was there with a bit of news about a colleague he had met for dinner. I responded with a brief synopsis of my day and then headed to bed.

The next morning, I started with a yoga flow designed to work on flexibility. I understand meditation is all the rage now and an important part of the overall practice. However, I've never been able to quiet my mind enough to reap its benefits. This morning was one of those times. As I dove forward from mountain pose to touch my toes, I found myself once again thinking about Lauren's

The Neighborhood

concerns surrounding 'the general's' death. Thirty minutes later, I brought my prayer hands to my third eye, wished the lady on the YouTube channel Namas Dei and headed towards the shower.

The internet repairmen showed up around 10:00 am. I took him to the office where our equipment lives and gave him a shortened version of the on-going saga that had begun about two weeks ago. Although I don't consider myself an anal person, I'd written down each time I went through the re-boot dance. Since the 6th of January, it had been eight times. He raised his eyebrow, said something about needing a new modem and began testing equipment.

Not wanting to hover, I went to the living room and picked up my copy of *To Kill a Mockingbird*. About twenty minutes later, I heard him mutter, "Strange". Thinking I should probably find out what was amiss, I went into the office and found him staring at a small rectangular device about the size of a flash drive.

"I found this attached under your desk. It may be causing the interference in your internet service."

"What is it?" I asked.

I could tell he was carefully choosing his words, "It's a listening device. I see them occasionally, you know, parents wanting to keep track of what their kids are doing or spouses checking up on each other."

"You mean a bug?" I asked incredulously.

"Yeah, you know it really isn't that uncommon." He was definitely uncomfortable with where this conversation could potentially go! Quickly, he finished installing a new modem, tested wires and then left.

I must have sat for thirty minutes staring at the bug in my hand. Why? Who? The repairman had intonated this was the kind of device used to check up on a cheating spouse. Well, I knew I had not put it there and in the deepest depths of my soul knew that neither had Peter. No marriage is perfect but infidelity had never been a concern for either one of us. We have too much respect for each other than to go down that path.

Not having any experience with devices like this, I turned to the internet to research surveillance gear. Although I had to use a magnifying glass to see the serial number, I was able to find it as well as the brand name. I typed the information into a search engine and found the apparatus in my hand was a pretty high dollar piece of equipment. As I was reading about the device, an ad popped up for a multi-functional bug detector and hidden camera finder. Although I am not paranoid as a rule, I added it to my on-line shopping cart and even paid for express shipping.

That night sleep eluded me as I tossed back and forth wondering who would plant such a device. The next day was not much better as I struggled to stay focused on class preparations. When I returned home from work, the package from the previous night's shopping was on my front doorstep. I quickly unwrapped it and read the directions. Thankfully, I had the right sized batteries! Carefully, I walked through the house. My search produced two more bugs, one on the back of our headboard in the bedroom and the other tucked under the bar in the kitchen. I sat at the dining room table with the three devices laid out before me. My hands were trembling. It didn't make any sense.

Channeling Nancy Drew, I decided to make a list of all the strange things that had happened over the past few weeks, trying to find a common thread. If being raised by a career military father had taught me one thing, it was to attack any problem strategically. First, I created a web of key events then, using post it notes, I add details of things I had seen or heard that may or may not be related. Key events included the break in at DFU and attack on Min, 'the general's' death and the bugs in my house. Two hours later, I had what looked like the conspiracy theory boards you see in the movies often created by an eccentric character. I wasn't sure if I was crazy or if I had clarity, but one name kept surfacing, Kevin Crank.

I sat looking at the board for a long time trying to decide what to do. Kevin did not strike me as a domestic threat. Perhaps it was (as my mother would say) his boyish good looks. He just seemed too wholesome. But appearances can be deceiving. How I wished Peter were here to either confirm what I was thinking or talk me off the ledge. There was no way to communicate through e-mail everything I had before me. Besides, what if our e-mails were bugged as well? It was still five days until Peter returned. I didn't know why 'the general' might have been murdered, but I'd never forgive myself if anything happened to someone else or to me.

After September 11th, the slogan, 'If you see something, say something' emerged. How often on the news had we witnessed some horrific act that might have been prevented if someone had just called the proper authorities. However, I wasn't even sure who the appropriate authorities were. After Lauren's experience with the police, I felt certain they would dismiss my suspicions. At this point, I was feeling pretty paranoid. Deciding I didn't feel safe calling this in from my house or even using my computer to research who to call, I got in my car and drove to the local library. Using the public computer, I researched the FBI's hotline to see if anything on my conspiracy board fell under their jurisdiction.

To my thinking, the break in and attack at DFU qualified as suspected terrorism. After all, they did work with the government on some pretty high-level research. The next step was to fill out the FBI's online tip form. I methodically went through documenting everything I had seen and heard. I must admit, I was feeling a little silly. But the burden of proof was on them. I was merely a concerned citizen sharing what I thought might be valuable information. At least that is what I kept telling myself.

After I clicked the submit button, I felt both relieved and a little embarrassed.

Pulling into my garage, I checked the rear-view mirror to make sure no one was following me and pushed the remote to close the garage door. Quickly, I got out, locked my car and scurried into the house, securing the door behind me. I made the rounds checking and double checking all of the doors and windows. As a last precaution, I wedged a chair against the knob of my bedroom door and prepared for bed. I slept a little better, but the nagging thought of who and why someone had invaded our home would not go away.

The next day boasted a sunny sky, a nice relief after so many gray days. In the light of this bright winter day, I felt a little silly about my suspicions of the previous night. Just then Kevin ran by on his morning jog. The shiver that ran down my spine was not from the cold. It could have been my imagination, but I felt his wave had a threatening tone. Rather than view my findings as the paranoid rantings of an AARP card carrying woman, I chose to see them as the wise observations of a seasoned lady. Embracing this positive self-talk, I headed towards the office for another day of class preparation.

The wonderful thing about having a job you love is that you can get so absorbed that everything else falls away. I spent the day reviewing the books for my class, revising notes and organizing my lecture for the following Monday's class. Before I knew it, the day was nearly over. I noticed a text from Jean, asking me to join her for an early dinner at our favorite Italian restaurant, Amore. Perfect, I thought. Dinner with a friend was exactly what I needed to balance the stress of the previous evening.

Jean was seated and had ordered a carafe of wine for us to share when I arrived. The restaurant's intimate environment and Tuscany inspired cuisine made for a relaxing dining experience. Over the years this had become a favorite spot for Peter and me to bring out of town guests, not only for the excellent food but also a way to share a bit of our adoptive state's history. Always the historian, Peter would give a brief history of Italian immigrants who settled and worked the coal mines in the early 20th century. The long-term benefit of this migration was bona fide Italian cuisine. Tonight, Jean and I chose to split an order of Eggplant Parmesan.

I wanted to tell Jean about my suspicions and report to the FBI with every fiber of my being, but decided it best to keep it under my hat until Peter returned. So, we spent the evening talking over DFU gossip and the upcoming beginning of semester cocktail party Jean and Randall would host. One of the perks people often talked about as being part of Deep Fork University was the collegial environment. No matter what department, you were considered a valued part of the team. Randall had really cultivated this culture and Jean had been a willing participant. Over the years, Peter and I had been recruited to serve alongside them as honorary host and hostess. Since Peter's position touched every department on campus, it was a natural fit.

After dinner, we got in our cars and I followed Jean through downtown and into the neighborhood. Whether you are traveling by car or utilizing the pedestrian bridge that connects our neighborhood to downtown, the trip is five minutes.

Jean honked as she turned into her driveway and gave me a wave. I blinked my lights, turned into my drive and pulled into the garage. The pleasant dinner conversation, wine and enjoyable day at work had eased my apprehension and helped me to relax. I was looking forward to a good night's sleep.

As I walked into the kitchen, I hung up my coat and bag and made sure to lock the door behind me. I turned to get a glass of water when I froze in my tracks. Sitting at my dining room table was Kevin Crank.

"We need to talk."

Chapter 7

When faced with a threatening situation, embedded within each of us is a fight or flight instinct. Mine was flight!!! Unfortunately, my feet were frozen to the ground and my heart was beating so fast and hard, I thought it would burst if I exerted myself at all.

Just then, another man came into view brandishing a badge, "Mrs. Johns, FBI Special Agent Spencer."

My first thought was, 'Wow, the FBI works fast' followed by, 'but why would you bring the suspect to my house?'

"I believe you already know FBI Special Agent, Ben Keith. Of course, you know him as Kevin Crank," continued Agent Spencer.

Sometimes when I pour cream into my coffee, I watch as the two substances collide and slowly begin to flow into one liquid. If someone were to do an MRI of my brain at this exact moment, I imagine that is the image they would find. The information I had just been given began to weave its way through the neurons in my brain until a coherent thought could be formed. Kevin Crank is an FBI agent.

I suppose watching my facial response was a bit like watching a movie in slow motion as I looked back and forth between the two men.

"Evelyn, you outed me," Kevin (Or should I call him Ben?) said.

"Agent Keith has been working under cover for the past four

months. The information you submitted to the FBI hotline yesterday has forced us to reconsider this operation," Agent Spencer stated in an accusing voice.

Kevin looked at Spencer and gestured for him to tone down his voice. "The allegations you made in your report were actually pretty accurate. I wasn't sure how you connected all the dots until I saw this." Kevin gestured to the collection of post it notes and strings. "There is just one flaw in your theory, me. I'm not the bad guy."

Up until now, I had not said a word. Agent Spencer gently took me by the arm, guided me to the table and pulled out a chair gesturing for me to sit. "I believe you enjoy a cup of orange spice tea in the evening, decaf of course," he said as he moved to put the kettle on and reached into the cupboard for a cup.

"How do you know…." My voice trailed off as the realization struck me like a lightning bolt. The FBI had bugged my house.

"Why?" I asked through the cloud of confusion that was circling my brain.

"In time, I'll answer all your questions. But first, you need some background," Kevin said kindly. "First off, it's quite unusual for the Bureau to take this approach with a civilian in matters of national security. But as we've stated, you already connected a lot of dots and the Bureau's determined it is prudent to include you in the loop rather than let you continue your own investigation."

Now that my brain was beginning to process everything, I realized what he was really doing was calling me a busy body.

"Excuse me!" I declared indignantly.

"Evelyn, I'm not trying to insult you. Quite the opposite. You're perceptive and intelligent. In the Bureau, that's considered a gift. But we'll get back to that."

"About a year ago, the FBI began gathering 'intel' about Russian sleeper agents operating in the United States. Apparently, before the Soviet Union collapsed there was a program curating and training agents to infiltrate the United States. These agents were in place when the Soviet Union dissolved. However, the program has remained intact. As Russia began to flex their muscles again, these sleeper cells were activated."

Agent Spencer handed me the cup of steaming tea, "We've been able to identify locations where these cells are placed. Some places are obvious, others not so much. Deep Fork University is one of those not so obvious locations."

He continued, "Are you aware of the quality of research scientists the Whiteley Research Center has attracted over the past decade? The research they are doing would threaten national security in the hands of our enemies. Becoming a DARPA center raises the stakes even higher."

I had always known the center was highly regarded and worked with the Department of Defense on various and assorted projects. However, I had never thought of the ramifications if the wrong people got hold of the research.

Kevin continued, "I was placed here to infiltrate the university and the neighborhood. As you know, many of the key players at the research center are your neighbors."

My gaze turned to Kevin as the impact of what he was saying rolled over me. "You thought I was a spy?" I asked incredulously.

"Not so much you as Peter. Remember when I asked you about the card from Dmitry Sergey? He has been linked with cultivating assets for Russia. His relationship with your husband as well as all of Peter's international travel put him and you on our watch list."

"We're not spies!" I forcibly shouted.

"We know that now. But we had to do our due diligence," Kevin calmly said. "Since I've arrived, the break-in at the university and Bill Walker's murder are cause for concern."

"Murder?" I shuddered as I whispered the word. Even though I had suspicions, I'd never said the word out loud. It's an ugly word laced with hate and callousness.

Acknowledging how this had shaken me, Kevin waited a few moments before he continued.

"Yes, murder. We're not certain it's related to our investigation, but we're not ready to discount it. Under our direction, the Deep Fork police department is treating it as an accident. We feel we will be able to move more freely if we have not raised red flags."

"Are you saying a Russian spy killed him?"

"That's our current theory."

"And you think this spy is in the neighborhood?" I could barely get the words out.

Kevin nodded affirmation.

"But these people are my friends." The nausea that had been building in my stomach welled up into my throat and I excused myself to go to the bathroom. A cold washrag on my face and neck helped to quell the sick feeling I was having. As I looked in the mirror, I felt as if I was looking at a stranger. The face looking back at me was drawn and fatigued. Overnight it seemed lines had deepened and I had aged immeasurably.

I returned to the dining room to find both agents patiently waiting, well at least Kevin seemed patient. Agent Spencer was obviously ready to move forward with whatever plan they had devised.

"As stated, Agent Keith, Kevin as you know him, has been sent to infiltrate both DFU and this neighborhood. His role as an IT person has opened the doors we need at the university. Unfortunately, he has not been as successful in the neighborhood. We feel that is where you can play a role."

"Sorry, I don't follow," I said in a confused tone.

"I need you to open doors for me, both figuratively and literally. I have to gain access to people's homes."

"Obviously, you don't need me to break into people's homes," I said wryly. "So, mine is not the only home you are going to bug?"

"Surveillance is part of it. But also, to move in their circles socially. You were able to pick up a lot of information not only through your observations but also through conversations you've had with people. I need you to get me into those circles."

Agent Spencer moved to the edge of his chair, "In addition, the Bureau would like you to be our eyes and ears. We need you to gather information, no matter how meaningless it may seem, and report it to us."

"You're asking me to be a spy?" I couldn't believe the words even as I said them.

"We prefer the word asset," Kevin interjected. "You are trusted by colleagues and neighbors. It would take me years to build those types of relationships. That's time we just don't have."

It was at that point I thought my head was going to burst. Obviously, the two of them were aware I had reached my saturation point.

"I know we've given you a lot of information. Let's call it quits for tonight, we'll be in touch in the next twenty-four hours to answer questions and discuss details," declared Agent Spencer.

"I'll need to visit with Peter about this," I uttered as I could feel a migraine begin to build.

The two agents looked at each other and Kevin said, "I'm sorry Evelyn, but this is for your ears only. Peter cannot be included in this proposition."

The Neighborhood

Well, if I hadn't slept well the last two nights, I knew for certain tonight would be even worse!!!

Chapter 8

When Kevin (I decided it was best to stick to the name I knew him by) said twenty-four hours, he was not kidding. Twenty-three and a half hours after the previous evening's revelations, my doorbell rang. Standing there was Kevin holding an empty casserole dish.

"In case any neighbors are watching. Gives me a credible reason for ringing your doorbell," he said as he walked in. For the casual observer it would definitely appear as a neighborly act. However, I was feeling anything but neighborly. Anger, astonishment, violation, nervousness and fear were just some emotions I had cycled through in the twenty-four hours since I had become privy to potential Russian spies among my circle of friends.

"I'm sure you have a lot of questions. Shall I put the kettle on?" It seemed quite presumptuous for him to be offering to fix me a cup of tea in my own home. Once again, a sense of violation washed over me.

"I think I'm more in need of a glass of wine," I countered. As I reached for a bottle, I turned, looked him squarely in the eye, "It feels wrong to offer you a glass. After all, this isn't a social call, however, the hostess in me doesn't want to be rude."

"Just water for me," he diplomatically said. "I calculated forty-five minutes is about the amount of time a neighbor returning a dish would stay so let's get started. "

I'll admit, this matter of fact approach was a little off putting but necessary, I supposed.

"First off, I don't like the idea of spying on my neighbors."

"Understandable. We'll only be targeting certain people, those directly and at times indirectly related to the research center. That eliminates a lot of your neighbors. There are five couples we've identified."

"Couples?" I was obviously confused.

"This particular program utilized by the Russians almost always uses couples. Obviously, it's hard to sustain a secret life style from a spouse over an extended period of time. Also, it's a double bang for the buck."

Over the past day, I had calculated just who might be on the FBI's list. If international connections plus access to the Whiteley Research Center were requirements, a few names readily came to mind. Both the Patels and Jungs as well as the center's director, Gary Barrett, met the criteria. I was taking a virtual tour of the neighborhood in my head, trying to figure out who else might be suspects when Kevin said, "The other two couples are the Andersons and Webers." I wasn't sure which angered me more, the fact that he had just named some of my closest friends or that I was so transparent he could read my mind.

"Now that is just ridiculous! Randall and Jean are some of our closest friends. There is no way they could be spies." I shouted disbelievingly.

"Randall's position at the university allows him access to sensitive information. The same with Victor Anderson. As Vice President of Research, he is aware of everything happening in the research facility. Again, we need to be prudent and thorough in our investigation."

"So exactly what would you have me do?" I queried.

"For starters, I need to plant a bug in each of their homes. Or one of us does."

My eyebrows shot up!

"Your role is to help me gain access to people's homes. In most cases, I'll be able to plant the bugs. We'll also need to meet regularly for de-briefings. We have about 30 minutes left for tonight's meeting. What else?"

"Peter. I won't keep secrets from my husband," I proudly stated.

"I know, Evelyn. In the brief time I've been here, I've watched the two of you together and admired your closeness, which also made you a little suspect," he raised his hand to quell my protest. "However, this truly is a matter of national security. The type of research the Whiteley Center is doing could be critical in protecting our military and civilians."

"The layman's term for the research program that will be part of the DARPA funding is Friend or Foe. Currently, bio-surveillance strategies based on biochemical markers fall short in identifying potentially harmful bacteria. The focus of this research is to develop a biological equivalent of Twenty Questions. Bacteria will be subjected to physical and chemical tests to determine whether it is harmless or virulent. You can imagine the ramifications of being able to detect bacterial pathogens as, or even before, they threaten the strength of the military and the health of the homeland, if not the entire world. Bio-terrorism is a very real threat. To have the technology to thwart a pandemic is major to the security of our nation. Ultimately, by serving your country in this way, you could help save lives."

Have I mentioned I'm an Air Force brat? My dad is a retired colonel. I spent my life on military bases throughout Europe and have an extremely high regard for our men and women in uniform as well as the families that support them. Of the voices in my head, my father's is one of the loudest. If he said it once, he said it a thousand times, "Home of the free, because of the brave!" From an early age my sister and I were well aware that we are all called to serve our country in one way or another. I just never thought it would be as a spy.

"You probably should have led with that," I grimaced.

"Your father had a very impressive career which I'm sure deeply affected your patriotism," he acknowledged.

"Also, there might be a time when it is advantageous to bring Peter into the fold. Just not yet. The tighter we can keep this circle, the better." Again, he seemed too cognizant of my thoughts.

"What else?"

"Evelyn, we're going to be spending a lot of time together, seen together. We'll need a plausible reason for our perceived relationship."

"Well, if our ages were reversed the obvious solution would be an affair." I could tell I had shocked him. "But I'm guessing you already have something in mind."

"I do," his voice was a little shaken, but he regained his footing. "Do you ever meddle in your daughter's love life? I'm thinking you see me as a good catch and are fostering a relationship with hopes of setting me up with your daughter."

I slowly took another sip of wine. Do I meddle in my daughter's love life? Now that was a difficult question to answer. No, I am not a mother who is always on the prowl looking for my future son-in-law. I certainly DO NOT voice my opinion to Lane about who she should date (after all, that would be the kiss of death). However, I have, on occasion, orchestrated a coffee or lunch date that happens to coincide with running into someone who might be of interest to my daughter. Hmmm, maybe I'd be better at this spy business than I first thought. But what Kevin was asking me to do was potentially use my daughter as a pawn. That was definitely not okay. I could feel my mama bear instincts kick in.

"My daughter is off limits," I stated firmly.

Just then an alarm sounded from Kevin's watch. "My forty-five minutes are up," he said as he stood. "We can just play this as a neighbor showing kindness to the new guy on the block. Are you in?"

Although internally every fiber of my being was shouting "No!", I heard myself saying, "Yes."

"Great. Tomorrow is Friday which means you'll be at the College Street Coffee Shop around 9:00. The temperature will be forty-five degrees, sunny, no wind. I assume you'll be walking?" I nodded my head a little taken back by his knowledge of my routine.

"I'll plan to arrive around 9:30. We can walk to campus together and discuss your first assignment."

With that, he exited my front door, gave a friendly wave as he walked down my porch steps and headed towards his house.

Chapter 9

One of my guilty pleasures is a café mocha. On Friday mornings, I give myself this little treat as a reward for either a week well done or a bit of solace after a rough one. As Kevin had observed, weather permitting, I'll walk to work. I don't know if I burn off the extra calories from the mocha, but I feel better about myself. Once, I calculated the distance from my house to the coffee shop and then to the university. It is under a mile. In the fall and spring, I'll often reverse the process in the evening. Otherwise, I catch a ride home with Peter. Tonight, I'd have to make a different plan to get home.

I was nearly finished with my beverage when Kevin walked into the coffee shop. I had my nose buried in my well-worn copy of *To Kill a Mockingbird* and pretended not to see him. Out of the corner of my eye, I watched him order coffee. Like an actor in a play, he turned and with a perplexed look tried to decide where to sit. Spotting me he waved and crossed the coffee shop.

"Good morning, Evelyn." I found myself wanting to applaud his performance.

"Hello, Kevin. I see you've found my favorite coffee shop." Sensing my voice was a little too high pitched, I lowered it and extended an invitation to join me.

"Thanks!" He draped his bag over a chair, retrieved his coffee and sat down. "*To Kill A Mockingbird* is one of my favorite books."

I looked at the book in front of me and realized we were going to be making small talk. "Mine as well. It's a cornerstone of the Race Relations in Literature class I teach."

And so, our chit chat began. I suppose a crowded coffee shop is not the best place for a clandestine meeting. For the next twenty minutes or so we visited about my course, books and local restaurants.

Without making too big of a show, we faked a realization that we were both on foot and headed towards campus. Together, we exited the coffee shop and headed north to the main campus entrance. Thankfully, the sun was indeed out and there was no wind. I found myself appreciating the brisk walk. It seemed to help defuse the anxiety that continued to worm its way through my thoughts.

"I understand the Webers host a beginning of semester cocktail party," Kevin cheerfully asked. "You'll need to secure an invitation for me."

"That won't be a problem."

"Also, I'll need to know where they spend the majority of their time while at home. I'll need to plant bugs strategically."

I suddenly felt dirty. I know the sense of violation I felt when I realized someone was spying on me. How could I do this to my friends?

Again, he was reading my thoughts. "Evelyn, we have to keep our eye on the objective."

"You do realize you're talking about some of Peter's and my dearest friends," I murmured.

We walked in silence till turning the corner and entering Deep Fork University. Although the spring semester did not start until Monday, there were already students and faculty populating the campus. I usually found the energy which surrounds the beginning of a semester stimulating. Today, I felt as if an albatross had been tied around my neck.

"When does Peter return?" queried Kevin.

"His plane arrives Sunday afternoon. He should be back here by 5:00." Perhaps the albatross was also carrying bricks.

"Evelyn, I understand this is hard, but it really is a matter of national security. Before Peter arrives home, we need to formulate a plan for how to infiltrate the homes of our targets."

I could tell he knew he had used too strong of language as my eyebrows shot up. "These are my neighbors we are talking about. They are nice people!" My defenses were definitely up. If nothing else, I would help him in order to prove their innocence.

"*The best spies are nice guys*," he said matter of factly. "In order to win people's confidence, agents have to be perceived as likeable. These sleeper cells are very well trained. They embed themselves into a fabric of a business, social group or neighborhood. The more they are accepted, the better their cover."

"We'll need to meet at my house so I can give you a briefing and train you on the surveillance equipment. This will take approximately two hours. I have not been able to develop a plausible scenario of why you would be at my house for that length of time, so we'll need to do this under cover of darkness." As he said this, he handed me an envelope. "This contains instructions of what to wear, when to arrive and other details needed for our meeting."

With that, he turned towards the Whiteley Research Center. Quickly stuffing the envelope into my bag, I turned in the opposite direction and headed towards my office in the Arts and Science building.

"Evelyn!" Jean was walking quickly to catch up with me. "What were you and Kevin talking so intently about?"

"We were talking about 'the general'," I threw out, trying to grab something that would come across as a plausible story. I surprised myself with how easy it was to fabricate a lie on the fly.

"His death has really effected all of us. So sad," she murmured as we each turned to walk towards our offices.

Throughout the day, my eyes periodically glanced at the envelope Kevin had given me. It seemed to be screaming from my bag, "Open me." However, I did not, would not allow it to overshadow the final preparations I needed to make for Monday's class. As I was packing up my bag at the end of the day, a few of my colleagues from the English department invited me to join them at the local wine bar. Every fiber of my being wanted to shout, "NO, I have to go home and study up for a clandestine meeting with an FBI Agent." However, acting normal and not spilling my guts at the first opportunity seemed to be a better choice. Besides, one of them could give me a ride home. For the next hour and a half, I sipped a chardonnay, shared holiday stories and chatted about the upcoming semester. By 7:00 pm, I was deposited at my front door.

Lane called just as I was opening the instructions from Kevin. Normally, I thoroughly enjoy calls from my daughter. I love hearing about her work, friends and whatever else she has going on.

"You seem distracted, mom. Is everything alright?" This wasn't good! If she could tell I was preoccupied over the phone, how was I ever going to pull the wool over Peter's eyes?

"Oh, you know, beginning of the semester and I am pretty tired. I may be coming down with a cold." Even I thought I sounded lame.

"Go get some rest. I'll call Sunday night when dad's home. I can't wait to hear about Barcelona. It looks incredible!"

Once again, I turned to the envelope that would serve as the springboard for my new role as an FBI Asset. Contemplating what drink would be an appropriate pairing with espionage, I considered a martini, shaken not stirred. Ultimately, I decided a strong cup of coffee (decaf, of course) was a better choice. Opening the envelope, I read the enclosed instructions:

Meet Saturday at 22:00.

Dress in dark clothing.

Follow your normal bedtime routine. Turn off/on any lights, television that you normally would.

Turn your phone to silent and airplane mode.

Exit through your back door. Do not use a flashlight. The Patels are usually in bed by then. Circle around their house and cross to mine.

If there are any cars or pedestrians, hide in the shadows until they pass.

Lights will be off at my house. Enter through the front door; do not knock.

Memorize this information and destroy the note.

I should have had the martini.

A quick search of the internet confirmed black is the only option when it comes to spy wear. Hmmm...form fitting as well. Obviously, this must be a young person's game. I avoid form fitting anything!

In addition, I discovered I should disguise my face with a mask. According to the world wide web, this could be done with a ski mask or one imitating an infamous character. I went through a mental checklist in my head and could come up with neither item in my closet. I'd just have to be creative when it came to covering my head and face.

Apparently, I should also have carabiners to clip to my utility belt as well as a climbing harness. I looked across the street towards Kevin's one story flat roofed house. I didn't think this was a priority at this point.

'A spy utilizes every part of his body for optimal tactical advantage. This includes his head. By wearing goggles, you can protect your eyes from dust while crawling through duct systems. A headlamp, on the other hand, can provide vital light without costing you a hand to hold it.'

Remembering the no flashlight instruction, I decided to tuck this information away for another day. Hopefully, I would not be rappelling down the side of someone's house or crawling through a duct system.

I read through the instructions again, set my phone alarm for the following evening and burned the note.

Chapter 10

Strewn across my bed was a plethora of black clothes for my first clandestine meeting. Fortunately, my wardrobe lay claim to a lot of black. I knew I was overthinking this, but it seemed like a good use of my nervous energy. I couldn't remember the last time I had given so much thought to putting together an ensemble!

With an entire day ahead of me, I decided instead of fixating on my wardrobe it would be wise to keep with my normal Saturday routine. I arrived at yoga class just in time for the opening breathing exercises. With my eyes closed, I breathed in slowly hoping with each exhale to release some of the anxiety that was growing ever since I'd agreed to spy on my friends. With two of the FBI's 'targets' flanking my sides and a third right behind me, I found it difficult to maintain focus. These three ladies had been my friends for years. We'd experienced a lot of life together. Kamya, Jean and I had shared the joys and challenges of parenting. Although Cynthia never had a child of her own, she always expressed interest in our children. As we each began 'the change', we laughed and cried as our hormones got the better of us at times. In fact, Lane had started referring to them as my Menopausal Mates.

After class, Cynthia noted I seemed to be having trouble with balance and asked if everything was all right. "I know if I have any type of congestion in my head it can really throw my balance off. Hopefully you aren't getting sick," she gently commented. Oh, if she only knew what was going on in my head.

"I have an ancient herbal tea recipe my grandmother would use to boost our immune systems as children. I would be happy to prepare a batch and bring it to your house later today," Kamya shared.

How could either of these sweet ladies be spies?

After yoga, I ran a few errands before heading home. As I was once again surveying my clothing options for this evening's meeting, the doorbell rang. True to her word, Kamya was delivering the tea along with her melt-in-your-mouth Indian shortbread cookies. They are a sweet, buttery soft cookie perfectly paired with a cup of tea. I made a mental note to take a few to Kevin this evening. No one who bakes this good could be nefarious, let alone a spy.

As per the tradition in our neighborhood, I invited Kamya in to share the delicacies she had brought. "No, no you must have your rest. You are looking quite tired these days, my friend. Are you not sleeping well?" Obviously, the answer was no. How could I be getting the sleep I needed suspecting that someone close to me was living a double life? Or was the real issue that I was about to begin living a double life? My head began to ache.

Kamya wasn't the only one to notice the bags under my eyes. Just this morning, I had done a detailed review of the bags and wrinkles I seemed to have acquired in less than forty-eight hours. Obviously my newly acquired double life was not helping with my anti-aging battle!

After I thanked Kamya for the delicacies and we said our goodbyes, I pushed the clothing to Peter's side of the bed and crawled under the covers. Perhaps a nap was exactly what I needed.

Surprisingly, I was able to sleep for a few hours and woke just as the sun was beginning to set. I still had a few hours before my assignation with Kevin. That would give me time to do a load of laundry, eat dinner, finalize my evening's ensemble...and of course fret.

Precisely at 10:00 pm, I opened the front door to the "Cranky" house. It was dark as I walked into the house, but Kevin's voice guided me down the hallway. As I carefully felt my way down the darkened passageway, a door opened to a well-lit room whose windows had been covered by plywood. What looked like closed blinds from the exterior actually served as a cover for a boarded-up window.

Rarely, if ever, have I rendered a man speechless with my attire. Tonight, was a first. Perhaps I had taken the head to toe in black a little too far. Starting from my feet up I was wearing black galoshes, yoga pants, a turtleneck, and mittens. Covering my blond hair was a black pashmina which I had wrapped around my head and face ninja style. For added warmth, I had grabbed one of Peter's suit coats. At the last minute, concerned lights from a passing car might reflect off my glasses, I'd added a pair of clip-on shades.

"According to the internet, this is appropriate gear for night surveillance," I said defensively.

Perhaps it was the pregnant pause before his response or the slight twitch of his mouth that told me my ensemble had rendered him both speechless and humored. Wisely, he chose to acknowledge my attention to detail and moved on.

The room we were standing in was obviously a bedroom currently being used as an office. On one side was a modest desk with a computer. On the opposite wall were bookcases covering the entire wall. Obviously, my friend the FBI agent was an avid reader. Although his home library impressed me, I was more than a little underwhelmed if this was the operation center for a major FBI investigation.

No sooner had that thought run through my head than, with a

gentle tug of the bookshelves, he rotated them to reveal a set-up which included a myriad of electronics, an FBI jacket and cap, Kevlar vest, gun and holster as well as an evidence board that covered half the wall.

There it was. Laid out before me, pictures of six couples, Peter and I included. Below each couple's photos were notes that included name, age, role at DFU, and in every case, a highlighted segment of information. I assumed this was the key intelligence targeting them as suspects. My eyes immediately went to Peter's and my photos. As Kevin had indicated, our relationship with Dmitry as well as Peter's extensive international travel had been our red flags. Fortunately, a big red X over our photos indicated we were no longer suspects.

Kevin stood quietly as I studied the board. I guess everyone has a past and as my mother would say, skeletons in their closet. Although I understood we ultimately would narrow the list of suspects to one couple, I had the uneasy feeling I might be learning secrets about everyone on the board. My level of discomfort was beginning to grow.

"Let's get started. As discussed, we began with six couples. You and Peter have been cleared, leaving five couples." Although his tone was matter of fact, I detected a sensitivity to my uneasiness.

"First up, Gary Barrett and Sofia Gomez. They're a little young to fit the profile but both of them have Russian ties. Originally from Colombia, Sofia's father served as an embassy attaché to Russia. After leaving that post, the family sought asylum in Toronto. An entry point for many of these sleeper cells is often through Canada. While Gary was at the Naval Research Laboratory there was a security breach, Russian hacking. Although there was never a connection made to Gary, it still raises a red flag."

"You said they were young to be considered part of this Russian Sleeper Cell training program?" I queried.

"Yes, but they may have been groomed for this role while they were still in elementary school. Also, he is in a very strategic position as Director of the Whiteley Research Center to gather information. We just can't rule them out at this point."

"Next are Randall and Jean Weber," he shot me a sideways glance as he pointed to their photos. "I know they are good friends of yours, but as you can see, there are connections we need to explore."

Although the information I saw before me was not anything I did not know, looking at it through the FBI's lens, I could see how concerns would be raised. Jean's grandparents had fled Russia in the 1920's just after the revolution. I knew from past conversations her family treasured and honored their Russian heritage. Information that was new to me was Randall also had a connection to the former Soviet Union. Early in his career, he had worked as an investment banker. During that time, he developed ties with banks in the USSR and made several trips to Moscow.

Next on the board were Manasi and Kamya Patel. Of all the intel gathered, theirs seemed to be the weakest in my humble opinion. While in college, Kamya had participated in an anti-USA demonstration in connection with the development of nuclear arms.

"Nothing associated with the Patels seems very incriminating," I observed.

"Manasi's work with Global Health Biotech is a point of concern. Although the organization itself does important humanitarian work, there are entities who could exploit their work. The research being done as part of the DARPA project, in particular, could be of value to some of these individuals."

Remembering the bag of Kamya's cookies I had tucked in Peter's jacket pocket, I offered them to Kevin. "I don't know how anyone who is busy spying could have time to bake cookies this delicious," I said with a little mockery in my voice. Kevin took a cookie and munched on it as I continued working my way through the evidence board.

Min and Jin Jung had a position next to Peter's and my photo. The big red flag on theirs was that Jin was actually from North Korea, not South Korea. I looked at Kevin with raised eyebrows.

"Jin's documentation has been doctored to sever ties to North Korea. Not uncommon for individuals who have defected, but it does raise concerns. Our intel has indicated we are dealing with Russian agents. However, North Korea is making moves to position itself prominently on the world stage. Infiltrating a facility like the Whiteley Research Center may well be an objective. Perhaps we have simultaneous operations happening."

"Finally, Victor and Cynthia Anderson. As vice president of research, he is privy to all projects associated with the research center. Cynthia's role as financial assistant to the president allows her access to follow money trails. We have not found anything in their backgrounds to raise suspicion. They are just positioned to have access to a lot of valuable information. Also, we have not been able to gather much information about them before they appeared at University of Toronto."

"I can't say that I can tell you much about their past. Victor is a man of few words, and when he does talk, it's almost always related to work. Cynthia is the extrovert of the couple. But not in a 'look at me' kind of way. She stays quite busy volunteering with several service organizations. She's a kind soul, a great listener and never makes it about herself." As I shared this information with Kevin, I realized I really didn't know much about their background.

The remainder of our time was spent developing a plan of how to plant listening devices in each suspect's home. Apparently, Kevin had been unable to do this during the day when most of the suspects were at work because of our active (he never said nosy)

The Neighborhood

neighborhood. He was delighted when I told him I was the keeper of neighbors' keys. In fact, I had keys to everyone's house on the board.

"Would a spy give me a key to their house?" It seemed to me sharing access to your home would be the last thing someone hiding a secret life would do.

"Part of the training they receive is to blend in, be part of the culture of their environment. If you are the go-to for picking up mail, feeding cats, etc., they would make sure you had a key. No doubt, any incriminating evidence would be secured in some way. My moving bookshelves are very rudimentary," he said gesturing to the bookshelves. "They would have a much more sophisticated system. In fact, if you can tell me which couples have done home renovations that would be helpful."

I had to laugh at this. "Most of our homes were built in the 1930's. Everyone has done something!"

"If you could put together a list of when, what was done and anything else you can remember about the renovation, that could prove useful."

As we finished what I thought of as Spying 101, I glanced at the Evidence Board. Along the right side of the board were a series of questions which needed answering. The one that I could not shake was 'Is Bill Walker's murder related to the sleeper cell?'

"How certain are you that 'the general' was murdered?" It was a question I had been afraid to ask but knew it was necessary.

"One hundred percent. Ninety-five percent confident it's related to our investigation," Kevin stated with confidence.

Again, I felt nausea mushrooming in my stomach. "So, one of these people. Someone I've called a friend is a murderer?"

"Yes, Evelyn, if our intel is correct, and I believe it is. This person would not hesitate to kill again. That is why we have to be very smart and careful about your participation in this operation."

I nodded speechlessly.

"This is a burner phone. My number is programmed into it as well as a direct line to the FBI. Use this and only this to call or text me. If I contact you on your regular phone, you can respond in kind. A key to our partnership being successful is to develop the façade that our relationship has grown. I know Peter returns tomorrow. Again, I cannot stress how important it is that you do not disclose any part of this operation to him. If and when it is necessary, I will give you clearance."

With that, he handed me my jacket and pashmina and informed me he would be escorting me home. We walked in silence as we retraced my steps from two hours earlier. As we approached my back door, I turned to say something. He quickly shook his head no, raised his finger to his lips, turned and disappeared into the shadows.

Chapter 11

I miss my husband when he is traveling. Don't get me wrong, I don't mind having time to myself. In fact, I usually enjoy time alone puttering around the house, working on minor projects or getting lost in a book, not concerned with routine or meal preparation. However, the house never feels quite right when he is gone. The companionship of having him near, to hear his breath occupying the same space and time as me is perhaps what I miss most. When Peter is here, it feels like home; when he is gone, it is merely a house.

Keeping with my normal Sunday routine, I attended church. When the pastor asked if there were any joys or concerns, I had to sit on my hands to avoid 'spilling the beans'. Afterwards, I stopped by the Corner Market to pick up a few supplies to bake banana bread. Not only was it one of Peter's favorites, but I also planned to take a loaf to Gary and Sofia. As per the plan Kevin and I had created, while dropping off a homemade treat, I would place the bugs in both the living room and kitchen. After the internet issues the surveillance equipment had caused in our house, Kevin changed to a less intrusive but equally powerful system. In addition, in three of the five houses we would be bugging, English was not necessarily the first language. The data collected at each house would be sent to a remote FBI site where agents would process and, if necessary, translate.

Sofia's smile was warm and welcoming as she opened the door. I accepted her invitation for a cup of coffee and we walked through the living room and into the kitchen. I was trying my best to appear normal, although my heart was racing a mile a minute. This would be my first covert mission as an FBI Asset. It felt as if every word I was speaking, every movement I made gave away the reason for my visit. Given all of my anxiety, I did not seem to be sending off any signals that alarmed Sofia. She appeared quite at ease as she busied herself brewing a pot of coffee. With Sofia's back turned towards me, I reached into my pocket and pulled out the first bug. I was able to adhere it to the bottom of the countertop as I nestled onto a bar stool.

Kevin had tasked me with accounting for each suspect's whereabouts at the time of the research center's break-in as well as the twelve hours between the last sighting of 'the general' and the discovery of his body. Once I shared this information with him, the FBI would cross check it with any other information they had gathered through phone records (and who knows what else). The idea was to find a discrepancy in the story.

Gary was, in fact, at the research center so Sofia and I settled on the couch as we drank our coffee.

"This is such an exciting time for the Whiteley Center," I stated. "My understanding is being named as a DARPA Center is an extremely big deal." I tried to keep my voice light as I took another sip of coffee.

"Oh yes! Three years ago, when Gary left his position at the Naval Research Laboratory to become the center's director, he knew it was a special opportunity. However, neither one of us anticipated something of this prominence coming to fruition so quickly."

"He's certainly made a positive impression at the university, as have you. Peter says you've become an invaluable member of the Global Studies Center. I'd say DFU scored a win/win with the two of you." This was not hollow praise; it definitely was the prevailing feeling on campus. I just hoped it was justified.

"I'm sure the break-in was quite upsetting for Gary." Okay, here I go! "Did they ever figure out the cause for it?"

"Strange as it seems, they have not been able to uncover anything. Gary and the police searched the building and checked the computers, but didn't unearth anything untoward. When Gary called to tell me about it, he was quite shaken up. I know there wasn't anything I could do to help, but I wish I had been here to support him."

"I didn't realize you had been traveling," I queried, hoping that didn't sound too nosy.

"My parents winter in Arizona, so I went to help them get settled."

"Oh? I guess I'd always assumed your parents still lived in Colombia. Where do they live when they aren't in Arizona?" As I said this, I hoped I was working from knowledge I had prior to last night's crash course with Kevin. Did I know Sofia was originally from Colombia?

"My family has not lived in Colombia since I was a little girl. We moved to Toronto when I was about ten," she offered as she broke eye contact with me and took a sip of her coffee.

"Wow! That seems like a huge move not only in miles, but culturally and climatically." Could I flesh out some valuable piece of information that would seal Sofia's guilt or innocence? I must admit I was getting a bit of an endorphin rush.

"As you probably know, Colombia is both a very beautiful and complicated country. My parents hoped for a better life for our family. My uncle lived in Toronto and offered to sponsor us."

Sofia seemed ready to change the conversation, and Kevin had warned me about pushing too fast too soon, so I followed her lead.

"Would you like more coffee?" She asked kindly. Aware I needed to plant one more bug, I declined the offer of coffee but asked to use the bathroom.

Sofia moved to take the coffee cups to the kitchen, as I headed towards the bathroom. Along the way, I placed the bug under a hall table. This would pick up conversations in the office, bedroom and living room.

We said our goodbyes, and I walked down the street towards my house. A walk that once would have given me a sense of comfort and continuity now filled me with doubt and trepidation. Although the FBI's goal was to unearth spies, mine was to find who had murdered my neighbor. It was not only the north wind that caused a shiver to go down my spine.

Using the burner phone, I texted Kevin that I had planted the bugs. I also shared the information I gleaned from my conversation with Sofia. He had stressed that although facts were important, I was also to share my observations and insights regarding behavior of the suspects. In this case, I shared Sofia's ambiguous comments regarding her family's relocation to Canada. I sensed there were components of the story she would not or could not reveal. I also suggested Kevin's team might check out her trip to Arizona. From what Sofia had told me, Gary was spending a quiet evening at home when he got the call about the break in. As far as I knew, there was no way to corroborate whether this was true or not.

Peter and I have traveled extensively and embrace the cuisines of the countries we visit. However, at the end of the day, a good meatloaf and mashed potatoes with gravy are the comfort foods we crave. Today, I definitely could use some extra comfort! Using Peter's mother's recipe, I began assembling the ingredients for meatloaf. Mrs. Johns was a devout Catholic who often referred to her sons as the 'Three Apostles': Thomas, Peter and Mark. She believed you should work hard, pray hard and have potatoes with every meal.

A few minutes after 5:00 pm, I heard a car pull into the driveway. The aroma of a peach pie baking met Peter as he walked into the house. We are not ones for public displays of affection, but when it is just the two of us, it can be a different story. Tonight, the welcome home hug I gave Peter was perhaps a little longer and more impassioned than he was expecting. Although my actions came from a deep need for the stability I feel from his presence, his interpretation eventually led us to the bedroom. I think we both benefited from some marital bliss.

A few hours later, as we were savoring the last bite of pie, the phone rang. It was Lane calling as she had promised. The next hour was spent with her on speaker phone as Peter regaled us with stories of his conference, colleagues and, of course, Barcelona. She was definitely her father's daughter as they discussed the architecture and history of this avant-garde city. The entire evening had an atmosphere of normality, a feeling I had been craving for days.

Toward the end of the phone call, Lane asked if I was feeling better. Peter arched his eyebrows as I assured her, I was just fine. After we said our good byes, Peter asked, "You didn't mention you were ill."

"I thought I was coming down with a cold, but I think I was just overtired preparing for the semester. You're the one who should be exhausted. Do you plan to go into the university tomorrow?" I queried hoping to deflect the focus off of me.

"I don't need to be there until the afternoon. What about you?"

"First day of a new semester so I want to get there bright and early. My class isn't till 11:30. Late enough the students should all be awake! Speaking of, are you ready to hit the sack?"

"Definitely!"

As we snuggled into bed, I felt relief that I really had avoided lying to Peter about anything this evening. Although I may have left out a few details surrounding my new career as a spy, I also had not been deceitful. Maybe I could do this!

Debbie Williams

Chapter 12

According to the roll, twenty-five students were enrolled, with another seven wait-listed for my class. Although this course was an elective, it met a humanities component required by every DFU graduate. Therefore, I consistently drew students from numerous disciplines. This created a context and climate for diverse and interesting discussions.

The syllabus required the students to have *Killers of the Flower Moon* completed by the middle of the following week. Between now and then, I would give a brief overview of racial history in the United States including slavery, relocation of Native American tribes, internment of Japanese during WWII and treatment of Muslims post the attacks of September 11th, 2001. Rather than dwelling on dates and facts, I choose to present this history through collections of letters and short stories written by those effected. My objective with the entire class is for students to "walk a mile" in someone else's shoes.

After class, I checked my phone and saw I had a voice mail from Jean. Secretly happy I had not been available to take her original call; I checked the message. She just needed to confirm what time I'd be able to come over on Friday to help with last minute preparations for that evening's faculty party. Good, I thought, I can take care of this with a text. Although I knew I couldn't purposely avoid people, I had decided to take care of as much business as possible through texts and e-mails. If nothing else, it gave me a sense of being in control of a tiny bit of this scenario I found myself living.

Confirming I'd be available by 2:00 pm Friday afternoon, I also mentioned I had invited Kevin to join the party. I received a quick response of a question mark. Don't overthink your response I told myself. Keep it simple.

Ran into him over the weekend and he seemed a little lonely.

There was nothing in my text that wasn't true.

I received a thumbs up in response.

Since both the Patels and Andersons would be in attendance on Friday evening, the plan was for me to text Kevin when each couple arrived. Then, using the keys I had given him, he would plant devices in their respective homes. On the surface this seemed like a simple plan. The challenge lay in what time each couple would arrive at the party. If they stayed true to form, the Andersons would be among the first to arrive. They were very punctual people. However, Victor often times would put in his time and exit early. Cynthia on the other hand liked to stay until the last guest left and then often offered to help the hostess clean up. The Patels tended to arrive forty-five minutes to an hour after the official start time of the party. Kevin would have to orchestrate his covert operation and own arrival to the party to coincide with their comings and goings. Thankful my part in the operation would be quite simple, I turned my thoughts to the Jungs.

Placing bugs in their house would be a bit more challenging. Although they would be at the party, their boys would be at home with a babysitter. Fortunately, an opportunity had afforded itself the night before. I received a text from Lauren inviting Peter and me to STEM Night at Emma's school. The Jungs' boys attended the same school and I was certain they would be involved in anything promoting science! Using the burner phone, I texted Kevin with this stroke of luck. We arranged for a chance meeting on campus so I could pass him my copies of the suspects' house keys.

I was finding all of this plotting and planning exhausting. A quick look into a mirror confirmed the stress my new occupation was taking on my face. I found myself wondering if the FBI offered spa compensation packages.

Peter had texted earlier letting me know he had walked into work and would need a ride home. Around 5:00 pm I saved the file I was working on and powered down my computer for the evening.

To anyone observing from a distance, what happened next looked like a chance meeting between two neighbors; however, it had been carefully timed and orchestrated. As I was crossing the campus to meet Peter, Kevin called my name. As he came up beside me, I happened to drop the book I was carrying. In a gentlemanly gesture, he reached down to retrieve it, deftly removing the envelope containing house keys and slipping it into his pocket. The whole interaction took less than ten seconds and looked totally benign. From my Spy 101 research, I knew I had just participated in my first (and hopefully last) Brush Pass.

"I've passed the information from your visit with Sofia to an investigation team. We'll have a clearer picture of her circumstances in the next forty-eight hours," he shared as we walked towards Peter's office. "I also wanted to reiterate it is imperative you not confide in Peter."

"Are you afraid I'll spill the beans within twenty-four hours of him being home?" I asked defensively.

I could tell he was choosing his next words quite carefully. "I trust in your ability to do the job I'm asking. You would not have been approached if the Bureau had any doubt about your intelligence and skills." He shot me a sideways glance to see if his diplomacy was working.

"However, you also have a very close relationship with your husband. My guess is that deception has not been a part of your marriage."

My steps slowed until I finally stopped. "Did you know we had a son? His name was Bobby. He died of leukemia when he was four." By the look on Kevin's face, I could tell this had not been part of his dossier on Peter and me.

"Losing Bobby was undoubtedly the hardest thing Peter and I have ever faced. Lane, too. The year following Bobby's death, all three of us did our best to hide how devastated we were. A different form of deception, but deception nevertheless. I guess we thought we were somehow protecting each other. It wasn't a healthy way to process grief. Fortunately, our pastor saw what was happening and reached out to us. As painful as the process of acknowledging and dealing with our grief was, we all came out the other side stronger. The three of us have a bond." As was often the case when I talked about Bobby, my voice began to tremble. The two of us walked in silence for a few minutes. "Yes, I am struggling with keeping this secret from my husband, but I understand why it is necessary."

"Evelyn are you sure you can do this?" His voice was gentle with undertones of kindness. I think it's the first time he saw me as more than an asset.

Before I could respond, I saw Peter heading our way.

I looked at Kevin, nodded affirmatively, put a smile on my face and waved at Peter. "Kevin is going to join us for dinner."

The Neighborhood

Chapter 13

My role at DFU is as an adjunct instructor, which basically means it is a non-tenure track position. Since I had no desire to pursue a doctorate nor did I have a bent towards research, I terminated my education at the master's level. My position allows me to teach a course I love, guide and mentor students at a critical time in their lives and have freedom to pursue other interests and, of course, travel. Since I had no class or office hours on Tuesdays, I was able to attend a noon yoga class. As was the case on Saturday, I anticipated seeing both Kamya and Cynthia 'on the mat'. Today however, only Kamya was in attendance.

"It's not like Cynthia to miss class," I observed after we wished each other namaste and were rolling up our mats.

"She has gone to St. Louis to visit her aunt. The poor dear had a fall and broke her pelvis. Cynthia is helping her get set up in a rehab center. Such a thoughtful soul, our Cynthia." Kamya always had a kind word to say about people.

"Cynthia has been quite dedicated to her aunt over the years. However, I don't recall her ever visiting Deep Fork. Have you ever met her aunt?" I asked hoping my question did not appear overtly nosey.

"No, I have not. I have always believed she regards Cynthia as a daughter. It must be difficult to grow old and not have children. But I suppose Victor and Cynthia will be in the same position at some point. It is surprising they never had children. Cynthia would have been a wonderful mother."

"Cynthia definitely has a caring nature," I agreed. Using this conversation as a springboard, I saw an opportunity to reflect on 'the general's' death.

"I've been thinking a lot about Jo. I'm so glad she has her daughters to lean on since Bill's death. I wouldn't be surprised if she ends up moving to Oklahoma City to be closer to both of them."

"Being close to family is very important to heal the heart," Kamya wisely stated.

"I know it is ridiculous, but I've felt a little guilty that I did not see 'the general' out the evening he died. Perhaps if he had spent a little longer talking to a neighbor, he wouldn't have taken the path by the creek so close to dusk." This was not a bald-faced lie. I did wish I had seen him that evening and perhaps diverted him from whatever path had led to his death.

"I did see him that evening," Kamya shared sadly. "I waved at him through the kitchen window as he rounded the corner. I knew Jo was out of town and thought I should invite him for dinner. But Manasi and I had planned to meet at the Peking Duck. Oh, if only I had invited him along, he might be alive today." Her words were laced with sadness and remorse. Again, I wondered how such a caring woman could be part of an FBI investigation.

I gently squeezed her hand as we exited the yoga studio together.

"Peter, hurry up! We're going to be late," I admonished as I grabbed my coat. I had arranged to meet Lauren, Matthew and the girls in the elementary school gym at 6:30 pm. Although the school was just down the street, I was anxious to get there. The sooner I could verify the Jungs' presence, the sooner I could text Kevin the coast was clear for him to plant the bugs.

The Neighborhood

During my crash course with Kevin in Spying 101, I'd asked if the FBI needed warrants to plant these bugs. The idea of random surveillance really bothered me. He assured me the proper procedures had been followed. Since research at the Whiteley Center was connected to the Defense Department, any leaks would be considered a matter of national security. Warrants had been issued for all six houses, mine included.

We arrived at the crowded gymnasium at 6:30 pm on the dot. Punctuality is very important to me, definitely a result of being reared by a father in the military. Tables were organized in rows filling the gymnasium. Beginning in second grade, students were given an opportunity to work as individuals or groups to create a science project. Each class also created an interactive experiment for people attending the fair. That way all students had an opportunity to participate at some level. As one would imagine, being in a university community with a strong science focus, parents highly encouraged their children to participate. Emma and Hannah were wide eyed, and a little shy, as they each held one of their mother's hands.

Our first stop was the volcano challenge. I'm always amazed at the pure joy the mixing of baking soda and vinegar can generate. As the girls' poured vinegar and drops of food coloring into the paper mâché volcano they squealed with delight as 'lava' poured forth. Their bashfulness seemed to dissolve as they excitedly pulled all of us to the next activity.

The fourth-grade classes had joined forces to create a variety of activities dedicated to the exploration of bubbles. I love bubbles! There is a lot of science to be learned but I just find them joyful. I don't care if you are one or a hundred and one, bubbles can make you smile. Therefore, I was not surprised when we found Miss Essie standing in a wading pool, enveloped in a bubble wall, grinning ear to ear. Peter offered his arm to help steady her as she stepped out of the pool and put on her fluorescent orange sneakers.

"Guess we're never too old to learn," Peter offered, mirroring Miss Essie's grin.

"Age is of no importance unless you're a cheese," Miss Essie replied emphatically. With a wave good-bye she donned a Cossack style hat and eagerly moved towards the slime station.

Although I was truly enjoying our time with the girls, I was painfully aware of my ulterior purpose. I continued scanning the crowd in search of the Jungs. No doubt Mee would be manning a table with his own experiment. Sure enough, two rows over I saw the family clustered around a table. The trifold display had the caption "Which Fruits or Vegetables Conduct Electricity?"

I had pre-programmed an 'all clear' text on my burner phone to Kevin so all I would need to do is hit the send button, which I did. With my part completed, I was able to at least partially relax and enjoy the time with the girls. I'm not sure who enjoys our role as surrogate grandparents more, Peter or me. Those two little munchkins definitely have him wrapped around their little fingers. Currently, Matthew and Peter were making paper airplanes the girls could propel using a makeshift launching pad. The aspiring aerospace engineers clapped excitedly when one of the planes soared through the hula hoop target.

As we continued moving from experiment to experiment, I kept an eye on the Jungs. The closer we got to Mee's display, the more nervous I became. Although my evening's assignment was fairly benign, I could feel my heartrate begin to accelerate. I took a few deep, calming breaths to try and control my anxiety. As we approached the Jungs, I checked my burner phone hoping for an all clear. No message.

Fortunately, the focus of the evening was on the displays created by the students. This allowed me an opportunity to focus on Mee and not the fact that his parents might be enemy spies.

"Mee, this is a very interesting display. I don't believe I knew fruits and vegetables conduct electricity. Could you please explain to me how this happens?" My request was sincere. I don't believe in offering false praise or pandering to children. Also, I really did

The Neighborhood

want to understand the science behind his project.

As I expected, Mee gave a step by step (and no doubt scripted) explanation of how the process worked with Jin and Min watching attentively. I remember the first time I heard the term 'Tiger Parent'. Immediately I had thought of the Jungs. I've never doubted their love for their children, but striving for excellence permeates their relationship. They definitely hold high standards for their boys academically.

Once we were thoroughly schooled in the conductivity of fruit, we continued to travel through the exhibits deciphering secret messages, viewing models of the human body and exploring ways to learn about weather, plus much more. Although my anxiety was somewhat diminished, I continued to keep a watchful eye on the Jungs and found myself musing over their parenting style. I always assumed it was somewhat culturally based. However, I now found myself wondering if there was more to it than that. Although the boys were active in sports and school activities, they were not ones to "hang out" with the neighborhood kids. It had always seemed to me they had a very controlled and protected life. If I was a spy, is that how I would structure my family life?

We were moving down the last aisle when I noticed Jin and Min engaged in a very animated conversation. Jin seemed to be checking something on his phone as he turned and hastily left the gymnasium. My heart skipped a beat as I reached for the burner phone in my pocket, and excused myself by claiming I needed to go to the bathroom. Heading that way, I brought the phone to my ear. The walk from the school to the Jungs' house was less than five minutes. I wasn't sure if that is where Jin was headed but if Kevin was still there, he would have very little time to make his exit.

Kevin picked up on the second ring. "Jin just left the school. If he's headed home, he'll be there any minute."

"Thanks, talk later." With that, he hung up.

As I stood in front of the bathroom mirror, my face ashen and my heart pounding, I thought to myself, 'pull yourself together'. Just then, the bathroom door opened and Min walked in. Our eyes met in the mirror.

"Are you okay, Evelyn? You're white as a ghost."

"Just felt a little light headed and thought I'd splash some water on my face." All which was true! "Mee did an excellent job on his project."

"It was an acceptable experiment for an eight-year-old. Next year's project will be more sophisticated." Although her tone was matter of fact, I sensed pride in her voice.

I was feeling a little braver so I ventured on. "I noticed Jin leaving. Do you need help getting Mee's project home?" I offered in a neighborly tone.

Just then her cell phone buzzed indicating she had a text. She looked a bit puzzled as she read the message and then accepted my offer for help.

Peter and I, along with Lauren's family, helped pack up Mee's project and our processional made the short trip to the Jungs' house. Jin was standing in the doorway as we made our way up the front steps. "Thank you so much for your help," he said as he took the crate of supplies out of Peter's hands.

Goodbyes were quickly said and everyone headed to their respective homes. After all, it was a school night.

Peter was still a bit jet lagged so by 9:00 pm he was fast asleep. Still on a bit of an adrenaline rush, I texted Kevin and asked if he could meet.

Repeating my steps from before, I entered his darkened house. Although I was still head to toe in black, my costuming was not quite as extreme.

"Were you able to get the bugs planted?" I asked as I shed my coat and hat.

"Yes. They have a pretty sophisticated security system. I had to be walked through disarming it by one of the Bureau's security experts. Apparently while I was resetting it, something was triggered which alerted Jin. Thanks to your warning, I was able to finish the reset and hide in the shadows just as he got home. "

"Does that type of security system make them more suspicious in your eyes?" I queried.

"Yes and no. It does raise a red flag. But you'd be surprised how many people have high-end security systems. What happens next is the real question. If they do a sweep for bugs, that tells me they are sensitized. The equipment is active so if it is not disarmed, we will be able to pick up on any conversations they have regarding the incident."

"How soon will we know?" I really didn't want this family to be implicated in anything dire.

"They speak Korean at home so it will have to go through an interpreter. I should have a report in the morning. Do you have anything else for me?"

"You've asked me to share things that seem off or interesting. None of this is incriminating as far as I can tell." I continued, "The Patels dined at Peking Duck the evening of 'the general's' death. She mentioned she had seen him walking past their house prior to leaving for the restaurant. Cynthia Anderson is visiting an aunt in St. Louis. She should be back by Friday. Finally, the Jungs' parenting style is very authoritarian."

I had decided to state everything with as little subjective information as possible.

"Okay, let's start with the Patels," Kevin said. "Do they eat out often?"

"No, not really. Kamya is an excellent cook."

"So, this is a bit of an anomaly in behavior. However, it will be easy enough to check out their credit card records."

"If they used a card. They are one of the few couples I know who tend to pay with cash."

"Duly noted. We have other ways of verifying their presence at the restaurant. Can you give me an approximate time that you think they were there?" I did my best to satisfy his request.

"Tell me about Cynthia's aunt in St. Louis."

I shared with him everything I knew about their relationship, although I did not have her name.

"It's not unusual for spies to have handlers in different cities. This is definitely something we'll need to explore. If you can get me a name, that would be helpful. Now, why did you include the comment about the Jungs' parenting style in your report?"

"Perhaps I am imposing my values onto this, but it just feels autocratic. I just thought if I was a spy, that is how I would build a relationship with my child."

"Hmmm," was all I got.

As I was putting on my coat, Kevin handed me a small can of pepper spray. "Just a precaution." A chill ran down my spine as I was reminded of the gravity and danger of what I was doing.

We agreed to meet for lunch after my class and he escorted me home.

I disrobed and crawled into bed comforted to have my husband by my side. As I adjusted my pillow and snuggled up next to his warm body, he murmured, "I love you, Ev."

Chapter 14

Within walking distance of DFU campus were several options for dining. Kevin had texted me earlier to meet at a local sandwich shop, Two Brothers. As I entered the restaurant, I realized why he had chosen it. Lining one side of the dining area were tall booths. Although you were in the middle of a crowded room, there was a sense of seclusion within the booth. It also offered a barrier for anyone eavesdropping on a conversation. Funny how I was suddenly seeing my world through a different lens. Anyone seeing us would view two neighbors enjoying a casual lunch together, as opposed to a strategy meeting between FBI colleagues.

"Any recommendations?" Kevin asked as he studied the menu.

"You really can't go wrong. The brothers who own the shop came from the east coast, thus the name Two Brothers. The menu reflects the ethnic diversity of their Bronx neighborhood. I love their Reuben and Peter's favorite is the meatball sandwich. Not the healthiest lunch, but worth it."

Kevin chose the meatball sandwich and I stuck with my usual Reuben. Once our order was placed, Kevin began to fill me in on information he had gathered thus far.

"The Jungs were anxious about the alarm incident. Once they put the boys to bed, they did a thorough walk through of the house to check for anything missing as well as a security scan on their computer. Oddly, they did not do a sweep for listening devices."

"This seems quite incriminating." I could feel my heart sink. I hated to think of what might become of their children if they were indeed spies.

"So far, there has been nothing in their conversation implicating them as our suspects. However, it is alarming behavior. I have a team focusing on Jin's time in North Korea. Not easy information to uncover, but we will get it. Meanwhile, we'll continue to monitor their conversations."

"I thought the FBI only worked within the borders of the United States. I've been trying to understand how you gather information from other countries. Is the CIA involved?" I truly was trying to comprehend the scope of this investigation.

"The CIA is tasked with collecting, analyzing, evaluating, and disseminating foreign intelligence. Our agencies collaborate when it becomes evident there is a threat within our borders. Since September 11th, we have been more diligent in collaborating. It takes a little longer to pull together all the evidence, but when we do, the information is quite accurate."

Our order arrived which was good since I needed time to digest not only the food but the information Kevin had shared. My dad had at times expressed frustration at the lack of communication between military agencies. This is good, I thought. Shouldn't we all be working together?

"We've also received some information on Sofia Gomez," he continued. "While her father was an attaché in Russia, an uncle in Colombia was murdered by drug warlords. From what we can discern, this was an act of retribution because Sofia's dad would not build a connection with Russian drug dealers. Once Sofia's father finished his term of service, the family defected to Canada instead of returning to Colombia."

"So, this clears Sofia?" I asked hopefully. In my heart of hearts, I was hoping we could eventually clear everyone taking up space on the evidence board. Then my life could return to normal.

"It speaks well of her father for sure. Although Sofia was only ten when they made the move to Canada, I'm sure her uncle's murder left an impression. This type of trauma can turn people in unexpected ways. We still need to dig a little deeper into her background. We also had a break in our investigation into Gary's background."

I raised my eyebrows expectantly.

"Gary Barrett grew up in the Canadian foster system. Those records are protected, which is why it has taken time to complete his dossier. He was born Gary Statton to a teenage drug addict. They pretty much lived on the streets. He never knew his father. When Gary was ten, his mother died of a drug overdose and he went into the foster care system. From the age of ten to fifteen, he was in seven different homes. At fifteen, he moved into a group home until he turned eighteen."

Whenever I hear the statistics of children in the foster care system my heart aches. For a brief time, Peter and I discussed being foster parents. However, the wound of losing Bobby was still too fresh. I immediately pictured a younger version of Gary alone and scared hoping to find a new family.

Kevin continued, "His intelligence was his saving grace. In high school, a chemistry teacher took Gary under his wing and helped him get accepted to the University of Chicago. The teacher's name was Jason Barrett. As soon as Gary turned eighteen, he legally changed his last name to Barrett and moved to Chicago. We have not been able to find any Russian connection."

I thoughtfully chewed on my sandwich as Kevin shared this information. "Everybody has a story. Some are just more heartrending than others. I know you need to do a little more investigation on Sofia, but I think they are two people who found each other despite some pretty overwhelming odds."

"You're a romantic, Evelyn." I didn't sense any cynicism in his voice. "My gut tells me you're right. We'll continue to monitor their conversations just in case. So far, we have not picked up anything incriminating."

"Hello!"

I looked up to see Peter standing next to our table. Although he was smiling, I could see the questioning look in his eyes.

Kevin stood up to shake his hand and I slid over inviting Peter to join us.

As Peter settled into the booth he said, "Hope I'm not interrupting anything. It looked like you were having a pretty serious conversation."

Without missing a beat, Kevin offered, "I was just telling Evelyn about my divorce. It's not something I share readily, but today would have been my anniversary. I guess I was looking pretty low when Evelyn saw me. Your wife is a very good listener. You're a lucky man."

Peter squeezed my hand under the table, "Yes, I am."

The rest of the meal was filled with lighter conversation. As Peter and Kevin talked about the upcoming playoffs and who was most likely to make it to the Super Bowl, I pondered how easily Kevin had fabricated an alibi for why we would be together. Fortunately, his quick response had shielded me from lying to my husband.

Kevin finished his lunch and excused himself so he could return to work. As he left, he turned and said, "Thanks for listening, Evelyn."

Peter watched Kevin walk out the door and thoughtfully said, "He's an interesting guy. Although I had qualms about him when we first met, I'm beginning to like him."

One of the things I love about my husband is that he (as a rule) does not pass judgment on people. He takes his time getting to know someone, not in a nosy way, but slowly and thoughtfully. He genuinely listens as they tell their story and, as if putting together a jigsaw puzzle, gets a complete picture of someone as to their character.

"What were your reservations?" I asked.

"He seemed to be hiding something. Guess it was about his divorce."

And that was that. A lot of husbands would have probed for details about the divorce. Not Peter. He told me once, "I'm not a mind reader. If I need to know something, tell me." Which in this circumstance was a good thing. Although there have been times I'd wished Peter would be more talkative, this was not one of them.

Peter and I walked back to campus after lunch, each of us lost in our own thoughts. One of the benefits of a long marriage is the ability to share time in comfortable silence. I spent the afternoon thankfully distracted by class preparation. I was just doing an end of day e-mail check and preparing to shut down my computer when Kevin appeared in my office doorway.

"I may have put you in an awkward position when I told Peter we were talking about my divorce. This letter contains details so you won't have to lie to Peter if he asks any questions. Please destroy it after you read it."

With that he laid an envelope on my desk, turned and left my office.

Beth and I met the beginning of our junior year in college. I was working on a forensic science degree and she was studying pre-law. For me, it was love at first sight. Beth played it a bit more cautiously and held me at arms-length until the spring. She was pretty focused on her studies and career and did not want anything derailing her. I was never quite sure what changed her mind, but thanked God it had indeed changed. By the time summer came, we were inseparable.

We both graduated the following spring. Beth started law school in Madison, Wisconsin, and I headed to the FBI Academy in Quantico, Virginia. Our plan was to get the first year under our belt and then marry. After I finished my training, I secured an FBI position in Milwaukee. Beth transferred to Marquette Law school and we married during winter break. Everything was going according to plan.

I had done well at the FBI Academy, receiving the Director's Leadership Award. This success followed me to Milwaukee and I was tapped to help with a variety of covert operations. It took me away from home. A lot. Of course, I couldn't talk to Beth about what I was doing and I wasn't there to hear about her challenges and successes in law school. People say the first year of marriage can be the most difficult. I think we both decided to accept that explanation and plowed forward.

As she began her last year of law school, I could tell there was a seismic shift in our relationship. I requested to be taken out of the field. Even though I was home more, we seemed to grow even further apart. I kept telling myself her apathy towards our marriage was a result of stress and exhaustion. I thought once she graduated, we would find the balance needed to build a strong marriage.

Two weeks before graduation, she announced she had accepted a position with a firm in Memphis and would be filing for divorce. The next day I went into my office, requested a field assignment and within forty-eight hours was on a plane to Seattle. Six months later she was married to one of her law school classmates. They just had their first child.

That was three years ago. Since then, I've accepted every covert operation I could find and assumed any identity I was given. I don't need a therapist to tell me I have buried my feelings and not dealt with my divorce in a healthy way.

When I told Peter today would have been my anniversary, I wasn't lying. Normally, I'm able to dig into my work and ignore the date. If I were to take time to analyze my melancholy state, I would say it is because I have before me what a healthy marriage should look like. I'm sorry you are in a position where you must keep secrets from your husband. I promise you I will do my best to draw this investigation to a close as quickly as possible.

Sincerely,

Ben (Kevin)

Please destroy this letter after reading it.

After I read Kevin's letter, I stared out the window for a long time not really seeing anything. Eventually, I tore the letter into tiny pieces. I was truly saddened by Kevin's story, but at the same time felt deep gratitude for my marriage.

"Are you ready to go home?" For the second time in an hour, a man was standing in my office doorway.

I turned and looked at the man I had shared my life with for thirty years, "Yes, I am."

Chapter 15

As promised, I arrived at Jean's house around 2:00 pm ready to help with preparations for the evening's party. For the next two hours we moved furniture, laid out dishes, set up a drink station and did little last-minute food prep. Although the event was catered, Jean always liked to add her own touches.

Jean and I are like-minded hostesses. Although we occasionally enjoy organizing formal dinner parties, our preference is to keep get-togethers casual and comfortable. Since eighty percent of our social engagements involve each other anyway, we'd found teamwork paid off.

Today, I found my mind wandering as I quietly worked through the tasks Jean had assigned to me. To even contemplate there was anything suspicious about our dear friends made me sick to my stomach. I know the FBI had to follow any possible leads, but I truly thought they were wasting their time investigating Jean and Randall.

It occurred to me as I moved plates to the serving table, Kevin had not asked me to plant any bugs in Jean and Randall's house. After all, I had easy access, especially today as we were setting up for the party. I finally decided in deference to my close relationship with the Webers, he had decided to do the dirty work. This actually showed a lot of sensitivity on his part.

"You've been very quiet today," Jean observed as we put the finishing touches on the serving table.

"Just feeling a little tired. Probably a combination of the first week of classes and these gray days we've been having." All of which was true, as well as dealing with my new role as an asset in an FBI covert investigation.

"We're finished here. Go home and get some rest. As always, thanks for the help!" Her voice was cheery as she waved goodbye.

I chose my evening's wardrobe carefully, making sure there was a pocket for the burner phone. Tonight, I wore a pair of black slacks, a loose-fitting blazer (with a pocket), a lace blouse and ankle boots with a low heel. Stylish but comfortable. I felt confident in this assumption because Lane gave the ensemble a thumbs up when I had worn it on a recent trip to Dallas. Taking a cue from my ensemble, Peter added a sports coat to his jeans and white shirt uniform.

Peter and I arrived thirty minutes early to assist in last minute preparations. I was tasked with monitoring the food while Peter played host at the drink station. This allowed Jean and Randall to mingle freely with the faculty. Just prior to Randall taking on the role of president, a major renovation had been done to the Federalist style house, bringing it into the 21st century. What once had been a series of small rooms now flowed easily one from the other allowing for entertaining large numbers of guests. The kitchen and bathrooms had also been updated. Fortunately, it had all been done with great sensitivity, retaining the house's original 1930's charm.

As I had predicted, the Andersons arrived promptly at 7:00 pm. As they were unwrapping from the winter chill, I texted Kevin the coast was clear. Earlier I had reminded him that he would have less than an hour before Victor would head home.

Over the next thirty minutes, a steady stream of faculty and spouses arrived. Because of the role Peter played at the university, he interacted with almost every department. Therefore, we both knew a majority of the campus faculty and called many friends.

Among the third wave of guests to arrive was Kevin. I was a little surprised to see him appear so quickly. He slowly made his way to the food table where I was hovering. There were several people helping themselves to the tasty **hors d'oeuvres** laid out, so there really wasn't an opportunity for us to visit. Through mental telepathy, I tried to read his mind. It wasn't working. He was engaged in a conversation with a professor in the Health Sciences college and her husband who also did IT work for DFU. Nothing in his demeanor gave me any clues.

As I chit-chatted with friends, I kept an eye on Kevin out of the corner of my eye. He was certainly a social butterfly tonight. I noticed he made a point of visiting with Victor sooner rather than later. At 8:00 pm, almost on the dot, Victor grabbed his coat and said his goodbyes. As Victor exited, the Patels arrived. Although the Patels were somewhat westernized, Kamya still adorned herself in traditional Indian attire for special occasions. Tonight, she was wearing a traditional sari of deep reds and gold. It was beautiful, and as always, evoked gasps of delight from the female guests. Kamya definitely knew how to announce her presence without saying a word!

The mood in the room was light and enjoyable. Everyone was still relaxed from the winter break and not yet overly burdened with the stress of the semester. I was visiting with Kamya about her beautiful sari when Kevin joined us. He too admired the traditional dress and engaged her in conversation about her homeland. Others joined us and Kevin eventually faded into the background. At some point, I realized he was not to be found. Not more than thirty minutes after my observation, I noticed he was at the opposite end of the living room visiting with Jin.

Around 10:00 pm the first wave of visitors left. The Jungs were among this group as well as anyone who still had children and a babysitter waiting to be taken home. By 11:00 pm, all that was left were nine of the people who appeared on Kevin's evidence board, myself included. Although Victor was absent, Cynthia was still present and chatting with Randall and Peter. Sofia and Gary were sitting on the couch chatting with the Patels, while Kevin helped Jean move food to the kitchen. I suddenly felt as if I was in a game of CLUE! We were in the parlor, with a glass of wine. But who was guilty?

As was typical, Cynthia stayed after the other guests left to help clean. In the past, I'd always viewed her sensitivity and helpfulness as an endearing quality. Now I couldn't help but wonder if she had an ulterior motive. Or perhaps, I was just feeling guilty because I saw it as a prime opportunity to collect information about her aunt in St. Louis.

"I understand your aunt had a fall. How is she doing?" I asked as I transferred food to smaller containers

"Better, thank you for asking. Unfortunately, at her age any fall is potentially serious," Cynthia answered.

"Did she break anything?" One question at a time, I thought, uncertain what vital information I might be able to glean from this conversation.

"Yes, she has a fracture in her pelvis, thankfully it did not require surgery. Apparently, this type of break just needs time. I helped her move into an assisted living center to recuperate and receive physical therapy during her recovery. How are your parents doing?" It was like Cynthia to turn the conversation to others.

"Knock on wood, my parents are in good health. In fact, I'm going to visit them this weekend." This time I was not going to let Cynthia deflect the conversation away from her. "Is this your aunt on your mother or father's side?"

"It's my mother's sister. She never had children of her own, so in many ways I have played the role of daughter. We've always been quite close."

"So, you were raised in St. Louis?"

"The suburbs of St. Louis," she offered as she carried food into the kitchen. I distinctly got the feeling our conversation was over.

Jean came up beside me and surveyed the now empty food table. "Thanks so much for your help, ladies," she offered appreciatively, as Cynthia joined us. "It looks as if the guys have their own version of how to clean up the drink station."

Cynthia and I turned towards the makeshift bar to see Peter, Randall and Kevin emptying wine bottles one sip at a time. Randall saw us watching, raised a bottle and with a wink said, "Waste not want not."

"Kevin seems to fit right into this crowd," Cynthia noted. "I saw you and Peter with him at lunch the other day. It's lovely he is making friends. You and Peter are a welcoming couple."

I'd given quite a bit of thought on how to respond if and when a comment was made about my growing friendship with Kevin. I decided every lie should be brief and have an element of truth. "He seems lonely."

"Here, I thought you were vetting him as a beau for Lane," Jean teased.

I had to smile, "I think we both know Lane would not appreciate any match making on my part."

"I understand he went through a pretty difficult divorce not too long ago," Cynthia offered.

"I think so…" my voice trailed off as I looked at him thoughtfully. I could tell both ladies were waiting for me to share any details I had, but honestly, that felt wrong and invasive. Which was ironic since I was complicit in bugging both of their homes.

As I was making my middle-of-the-night trip to the bathroom, I decided to check my burner phone for any messages. Sure enough, there was a text sent around midnight.

When can you meet this weekend?

I'm going to visit my parents in Oklahoma City. Won't be back till late afternoon Sunday.

I'll meet you at a remote site on Sunday at 2:00. I'll text you details.

I guess spies don't get the weekend off.

Chapter 16

I am fortunate that into their late seventies both of my parents are in very good health. As my dad would tell you, "Result of genetics and clean living." Although I would never call my parents athletic, they have always stayed active, both mentally and physically.

Colonel Louis Cable enjoyed a distinguished career in the Air Force with overseas assignments in Belgium, Germany and Italy. Blessed with two daughters, I secretly felt my father would have preferred sons. Although neither my sister nor I were tom boys, dad made sure we developed skills of self-reliance. Road trip games included "what if" scenarios. We were questioned and coached on how to get out of a variety of compromising situations. My firm belief that everything is figureoutable is a direct product of these exercises. The expectation was always that you could and would take care yourself.

My childhood was blessed with 'seeing the world' as my mother would say. Wherever we were stationed, she made sure my sister, Karen, and I experienced the local culture and food. Many would call it a charmed life and I definitely have no complaints. Between my eight and eighteenth birthdays, I lived in Belgium, Germany and Italy. Karen often reflected our mobile childhood taught us to say hello and goodbye really well. As much as I valued my time overseas, a part of me always envied families who lived in one house their entire lives. I yearned for that type of stability. It's one of the many reasons I was drawn to Deep Fork and our neighborhood.

Dad's last assignment had been Tinker Air Force Base. He and mom fell in love with the laid-back atmosphere and kind nature of the people in this region. Knowing they could travel anywhere, they wanted roots where they could grow relationships, therefore choosing to retire in Oklahoma City. This also put them in close proximity to my sister in Dallas. Our decision to move to Deep Fork a few years later put them over the moon.

I was greeted at the front door with big hugs and smiles. Once I had put my suitcase in the guest room, they offered me a cup of tea and brought me up to date on their various projects. Dad was actively involved in the local food bank. Upon retirement, he had walked in intending to volunteer once a week. What he found were well intentioned people who needed someone to take charge. He was glad to oblige. With military precision, he helped re-organize their storage and delivery methods and recruited a retired software engineer to update their inventory system. It had served as a great transition from full time military to total retirement. It also gave him an audience, besides my mother, to listen to his sometimes-long-winded stories. For the first few years, he was there 20-30 hours a week. Now he volunteered two afternoons a week; the rest of his time was spent golfing, having coffee with friends and reading - a passion that had been a life-long connection for us.

Mom always had an artistic bent and in the past years had discovered a passion for painting with watercolors. She had transformed a bedroom into a studio which looked as if it was taken out of a Better Homes and Gardens photo shoot. Natural light filled the room where an easel holding her latest project stood in one corner. Beside the easel was a table neatly laid out with a palette, pencils, paints and brushes. Running along one wall at table height was a narrow shelf. Adorning this shelf were past projects as well as paintings in progress. Neatly organized throughout the rest of the room were books, knick-knacks and many, many family photos. It always made me happy to be in this space. Primarily because it brought so much joy to my mom.

We enjoyed dinner at a local restaurant and then came home for a Scrabble match. My dad never bought into the philosophy of letting your kids win games. Again, this was an overarching theme of his parenting philosophy that nothing would be given to us, we would need to earn it. Surprisingly, this is where my mom's competitive nature would emerge. Not so much when we were kids but definitely as we became adults. There was not a lot of chit chat as we each scrutinized the board looking for the smartest and highest letter count. Heaven forbid food should be put onto the table during one of our games. Peter has never enjoyed our family game nights. I've always assumed it's because it brings out the highly competitive, sometimes not so nice, side of each of us. The first time he was privy to one of our matches was early in our relationship. My mom was in the lead, dad was a close second and I was a distant third. At the last minute, I was able to play a triple-triple, the Holy Grail of Scrabble. I suppose most families would have slapped the winner on the back and congratulated them on such a rare play. Not Louis and Rae Cables. The obligatory congratulatory handshakes were given and then my sulking parents went to bed.

Dad emerged the victor in tonight's match!

The following morning, I attended church with my parents and, after lunch, headed back to Deep Fork. At least that is what my parents assumed. In fact, I was scheduled to meet Kevin at a hotel on the east side of Oklahoma City. I know it sounds sleazy, but it would give us privacy and time to discuss our strategy. Earlier, he had texted me the location and room number. I arrived a few minutes before 2:00 pm.

As I punched the hotel's address into my navigation system, I anticipated finding a run-down hotel with sordid patrons smoking cigarettes and hanging over balcony rails. Instead, I arrived at a bustling facility offering suites, studios and extended stay options. Apparently, there had been a youth basketball tournament nearby because the lobby was teeming with coaches, teenage boys and their families. As conspicuous as I felt moving through the lobby, I realized I was all but invisible. Not a single person made eye contact or offered a smile. My mom had once reflected as you become older people tend to look past you, more so for women. Apparently being a woman in your mid-fifties is a plus if you want to be a spy!

I arrived at the designated room and knocked. Kevin opened the door and I walked into what appeared to be a makeshift office. The room was one of the studio options offered by the hotel. It had a mini kitchen, table with two chairs and couch that could pull out to a queen-sized bed. I must admit, I had been a bit uncomfortable meeting a man who was not my husband in a hotel room. Although our meeting was by no means innocent, it was not the type of rendezvous one might expect at a hotel. Again, I thought it showed sensitivity on Kevin's part to choose the studio option. The business like set up allowed me to relax a bit. I exhaled a long breath that I had not even realized I'd been holding and took off my coat.

On the table sat a computer along with a portable file box. Propped up on the couch was a makeshift evidence board. Taped onto poster boards were photos of the information Kevin had collected. The boards included photos of the suspects, along with all relevant intel that had been gathered. I noticed additions had been made to each suspect's profile since the last time we had met.

"What time will Peter expect you home," he efficiently asked.

"I normally would try to get home by dark, so 5:30ish. It's an hour and a half drive from here, so I should plan to leave by 4:00 pm."

"Let's make the next two hours productive." And with that we began.

"I was able to plant the listening devices in the Webers', Andersons' and Patels' houses on Friday evening. Here are the keys you gave me."

"Don't you want to keep them, just in case?" I wondered.

"I've made copies. Besides, it might raise questions if Peter noticed the missing keys." Obviously, this wasn't his first rodeo. "Entering and planting the devices was very simple. The Jungs were the only ones with a security system."

"I found myself watching you throughout the evening. I guess I thought you wouldn't arrive until after you had planted bugs in both houses. It surprised me when you arrived before the Patels and then I barely noticed you disappearing after their arrival. I'm not sure what I expected of the evening, but I was surprised at how social you were. You really seemed to be having a good time. I guess I thought you would lurk in a corner taking notes on the suspects." I could feel myself beginning to ramble, something I do when I'm nervous.

He gave me a peculiar look, "You do realize this is my job. I'm not in it to be popular."

Obviously, I had offended him. "I just meant you were visiting with a lot of people that evening."

"It was important for me to be seen and heard throughout the evening. At some point, our sleeper agents are going to realize they are under suspicion and will begin their own analysis of who is investigating them. As the new guy, I will be at the top of the list. It's imperative my presence can be accounted for at key times."

"Moving on," he continued, "our goal today is to bring you up to date on each suspect, record any new information you might have and create an action plan. Let's get started."

First on the list were Gary and Sofia. "As I told you last week, we have not uncovered anything to raise further concerns. Although we will continue to monitor conversations, I'm ready to mark them off as prime suspects. Would you like to do the honors?" He asked as he handed me a blue marker.

"Is there any significance to blue as opposed to the red you used on Peter and my photos?" I asked as I drew a large X over Gary and Sofia's section on the board.

"Red indicates you are no longer a suspect. Blue indicates continued monitoring but not active investigation."

Next were Randall and Jean. "We've been tracking the Webers' travel over the past five years. They have traveled either to or through Turkey multiple times. What can you tell me about those trips?"

"As you know, Peter runs the Hanser Center of Global Education. When Randall became president of the university fifteen years ago, he and Peter crafted a plan to increase the scope of travel. Up until that point, most of the travel had been in Europe. Over the last ten years, the program has expanded travel to include Egypt, Turkey and Russia. In the next five years, plans are in the works to include travel to Asia." I could see Kevin's eyebrow raise as I ticked off these countries.

"Within each of these countries academic, humanitarian and corporate connections have been made. The center wants students to be more than tourists. At any rate, having the president of the university visit on a regular basis helps to build and maintain these relationships. Therefore, Randall makes at least one international trip a year, sometimes two. Jean often times will accompany him." As I was talking, Kevin was recording the information. Geez, even to me this sounded suspicious.

He next turned to the Patels. "They speak in their native language at home, so it is taking a while to translate what we are picking up. We've been following a Russian connection with Global Health Biotech. Shortly after Manasi stepped down as director, there were some funding improprieties uncovered. These led back to the Russian mafia. Nothing that directly implicates Manasi, but if there is any connection, we need to find what it is. Sometimes known as Bratva, these mobsters are bad news. Their modus operandi is to exploit an individual's vulnerability to get what they want. We'll continue investigating to see what we can uncover."

"By the way, we confirmed they did eat at the Peking Duck the evening of the murder," he shared.

"Does that serve as an alibi?" I asked hopefully.

"Not really. They could have committed the murder before or after their visit to the restaurant. If dining out is an anomaly as you indicated, it seems quite convenient to have their whereabouts documented the evening of a crime. Also, they did use a credit card. Another inconsistency in their normal behavior."

I involuntarily shuddered. "That seems very cold blooded. Kill someone and then order Moo Goo Gai Pan." The very thought of it sickened me.

Kevin paused as I regained my composure. "The Jungs are still quite agitated over the break-in. I've also noted some adaptations in their routine. The boys had been allowed to walk to school on their own in the mornings; a sitter picks them up in the afternoons. Since last Tuesday, either Min or Jin walk them to school."

"I can understand being overly protective of your children if you felt your home was violated," I said in my most motherly tone.

"Just an observation. As best we can tell, they have not called or attempted to contact a third party. Are you aware of any travel plans in the near future?"

"Not that I am aware of. Min's parents live in Michigan so they may have a trip planned there for the summer."

"We'll add gathering this information to your action plan. Are you aware of any connection to Jin's family?"

"No, I think I've always assumed they were dead. As far as I know, they have not traveled back to South Korea for any family visits," I said realizing how little I really knew about my neighbors.

"Finally, the Andersons. An interesting couple. We have not been able to pick up much conversation. It's like they don't talk to each other," Kevin reflected.

"Victor is brilliant and very career focused. Cynthia is the social one of the two. She spends a lot of time volunteering and works full time as well. Maybe they just aren't home," I pointed out.

"That's a plausible explanation. Just a different relationship than the other couples we are monitoring." I could tell my suggestion had not calmed his concerns. "Thanks for the information you sent me regarding remodeling and updates to the houses in question. You're right, every house has had something done."

"Was there anything useful in what I gave you?"

"Hard to tell. Mainly I'm trying to discern if under the cover of one remodeling project, someone was able to install a secret space. It looks like any renovations were done to the president's house prior to the Webers moving in. The other three houses have had some type of renovation done since they were purchased, usually updating kitchens and bathrooms. I'm surprised, living in tornado alley, that the houses don't have basements," he reflected.

"I can give you the short answer or Peter's answer," I offered.

"Educate me," Kevin stated.

"Because of Oklahoma's clay soil, the ground tends to expand and contract. This creates pressure on the concrete causing cracks, leading to moisture in the basements."

"Makes sense," Kevin nodded.

"Peter would reference Frank Lloyd Wright's desire to create a unique and affordable American house design. Wright's slab on grade, ranch style design was popular around the time our neighborhood was being built. Hence, no basements. Of course, after the big tornado ten years ago most of us put in storm shelters."

I could tell I had piqued his interest, "Those aren't on your list of renovations. Who has installed these?"

"Almost everyone who didn't have a basement. Both the Andersons and Webers, as well as Peter and I."

"What's the process for installation?" he queried.

"It only takes a day. A portion of the garage floor is removed, the ground dug out and the unit is dropped in place. They come in a variety of sizes."

Again, he was furiously taking notes.

We were running out of time so I quickly shared the little information I had gathered. I had been unsuccessful in getting much information from Cynthia about her aunt. "You know, it is funny to have been friends with someone over a decade and yet not really be able to tell you much about them. I never knew Cynthia grew up outside of St. Louis. I would have sworn she was from up north."

"Why do you say that?" Kevin asked pointedly.

"Mainly because she and Victor met at University of Buffalo. I guess I assumed only people from the north went to school up there."

"Anything else?" I sensed he was not overly impressed with my power of deduction.

The last thirty minutes of our meeting was used to create an action plan for me.

1. Find out if the Jungs' have travel plans.
2. Learn more about Min's and Jin's families.

3. Continue to seek opportunities to converse with the Jungs. Specifically, see if they mention the break-in.
4. Gather additional information about Cynthia's St. Louis aunt.
5. Talk with Peter about overseas connections, especially, those connected with Randall. *I did not like including my husband in this covert operation.*
6. Patels – see if there is anything that would make you think they are being coerced to working with Russian mafia. Family in India? Health issues??

Leaving Oklahoma City, I headed east towards home thankful I had the next hour and a half to ponder on my meeting with Kevin. I have always considered myself a trusting soul, thinking the best of people. Now, I was examining every conversation and second-guessing every action our suspects made. With a start I realized I no longer viewed these people as friends and neighbors, but as potential villains.

Chapter 17

For once, the weather station's prediction proved correct. By Tuesday morning, a thin sheet of ice-covered streets and sidewalks caused the cancellations of school, including Deep Fork University. Sleet continued to fall till mid-afternoon, ensuring a second day of cancellations. Anticipating a couple of days of being homebound, Peter and I, as well as everyone else in Deep Fork, stocked up on comfort foods for the duration. As a born and bred Minnesotan, Peter always scoffed at the southern panic over a weather event such as this. I, however, embraced it whole heartedly as an opportunity to wear my comfiest clothes - yoga pants and a should-have-been-thrown-out-five-years-ago sweatshirt. But it was just the right weight and never seemed to be too small, even when everything else in my wardrobe apparently was shrinking. I also had a pair of fuzzy socks in bright pink that Lane had given me when she was about ten. Not a fashionable look, but oh so comfortable. Needless to say, makeup was taboo.

The action list Kevin had given me was weighing on my mind. Being housebound was obviously putting a damper on my social interactions but provided ample time to question Peter. I was crafting an opening line that would appear natural yet evoke the information I needed, when Peter gave me the perfect opening.

"Ev, want to talk about our summer travels?" My unsuspecting husband asked.

"Sounds like a perfect way to spend an icy, winter day! Why don't you start a fire and I'll put on a pot of coffee." I figured the more relaxed environment I could create, the better I'd feel about my covert interrogation (which is what it had become in my mind).

This summer, Peter would be leading thirty students and two other faculty on the Architectural History: Art, Science and Culture Program. This six-week program, which began in Paris, would include Rome, Greece and finally Istanbul. Although I occasionally joined Peter for the entire trip, we discovered it was more fun to meet toward the end, then take off on our own adventure. Traditionally, I joined him as students left. He would take a few days to rest and I would explore the city on my own. Afterwards we would head into the countryside to explore small villages, hill towns, vineyards and seaports. More often than not, Lane joined us for our travels.

The addition of Istanbul to the itinerary had been a last-minute directive from Randall. In recent years, connections had been groomed to make this a viable stop for the program. Unlike many travel abroad programs, DFU students rarely stayed in hotels. Whenever possible, they stayed in dormitories, public housing or homes of locals. This broadened the cultural understanding of the students as they experienced what "home" looked like in different countries. Although it could be a headache for Peter and his staff, it definitely enriched the students' overall experience. With Randall's help, Peter had created a partnership with a small university located in the heart of Istanbul. A robust public transport system including boats, subways, buses and trams allowed the students to move easily throughout the city.

"The inclusion of Istanbul has been a nice addition to the program," I commented as I stirred creamer into my coffee. I had vowed I would keep any comments or questions I directed towards Peter honest. If and when this all came to light, I did not want my husband to feel used or betrayed. After all, I was leading a double life. But maybe that would actually add some spice to our marriage. My mind began to wander to a scenario where I was wearing a trench coat, fedora and little else. FOCUS! No time to go down that path…yet.

"Definitely," Peter agreed. "Although I had not included it in this year's itinerary because of cost, it looks like Randall was able to pull some strings and get housing at a very affordable rate. Istanbul as the final destination of the program is a significant component in expanding the students' world view. So many students think culture began with the Renaissance."

With that began an hour-long lecture which included Greek gods, the rise and fall of the Roman Empire, Constantinople's (current day Istanbul) glory days of art, culture and science as well as the emergence of our current day liberal arts education through France's Cathedral Schools. I'm smarter for having spent thirty years with Peter. Although architecture and history are his passion, he does not limit his curious nature to those subjects. He is a life-long learner and is constantly researching and gathering information to broaden his knowledge base. I could see why the architectural history class he taught each fall was standing room only. Even students who were not able to take it for credit would occasionally drop in. The class was also audited by many people in the community planning a trip overseas. Peter's lectures always included politics, religion, espionage, sex (without being salacious) and scandal. That was his hook. But in the end, he pulled it all together and connected the dots to give the listener a richer understanding of why a certain building was key to understanding the history of a culture.

I refilled both of our coffee cups as he finished with "... and that is why Istanbul is an important experience for the students."

"Well done, Professor Johns," I teased him. "So how did Randall develop these Istanbul connections?" I really was curious.

"Funny enough, that story actually includes Jean. When Randall was dean of the business college in Kentucky there were two students from very wealthy Turkish families. I'm not sure how, but at some point, these students discovered when Jean's ancestors fled Russia during the revolution, they had done so via Turkey. However, the coincidence that sealed their relationship is that

Jean's grandfather, who was a physician, had practiced medicine with one of these young men's great grandfather. The family in Turkey got news of this connection. Being a culture that values family, they embraced Jean and Randy as part of theirs. It has turned out to be a very fortunate relationship on many levels. In fact, Jean and Randy will join us in Istanbul and stay with the family."

"It really is a small world," I'm not even sure I said it aloud. Although it was a heartwarming story, I found myself questioning whether or not it was true. I hate doubting my friends!

"Although we'll spend a few days with Randall and Jean in Istanbul, I doubt we'll do any extensive travel with them this time. Which brings me to ask, where do you want to go, Ev?"

"It's been such a gray winter, anywhere with sun sounds good to me," I stated truthfully.

"Sounds like the Mediterranean Coast to me. You haven't been to Greece in several years."

"Exactly, what I was thinking. I think Lane was fifteen the last time we were there."

The next few hours were spent reading old travel books, perusing on-line sites and putting together a reading list for fiction and non-fiction books that take place in Greece. The book list was a tradition started by my mother when we lived overseas. Wherever we were stationed, she had us read books located in that region. It helped to enrich our experience as we explored cities, traveled through the countryside or visited an abandoned castle. This tradition is now interwoven into our family's DNA. Lane does it, as well as my sister Karen and her two step-children. Travel and reading are the common threads unifying our family.

At some point, Peter got absorbed in a book and I drifted off to the bedroom. I dug the burner phone out from under my socks and typed in the information regarding Jean's grandfather and the

Turkish connection. Once again, I found myself wondering about the plausibility of this story. Stranger coincidences had happened, but still it seemed pretty shaky.

I received an immediate response from Kevin,

Do you know Jean's grandfather's surname?

Oddly enough, I did. On a recent outing to Tulsa, we had stopped at a pub that boasted over a hundred international beers. Jean had commented that the Russian beer, Baltika, was spelled the same as her family name.

Baltika

I'll start investigating. The ice storm is thwarting our investigation. Can you arrange a dinner party for Friday night that includes me, Webers and Andersons?

I was curious what information he hoped to gain but sent an affirmative response.

Jean and Randall were a no-brainer. Victor and Cynthia were not typical dinner guests at our house. Not for any particular reason, Peter and I had just never clicked with them as a couple. However, I sensed they were both socially astute enough to see the value in being included in an intimate dinner party that included the president of DFU. Even though Cynthia worked in Randall's office, I suspected she did not see herself as Randall's social equal. I often had wondered if that is why she joined so many committees and organizations, trying to climb the social ladder for lack of a better term.

I floated the idea to Peter. He raised his eyebrows when I mentioned Cynthia and Victor but agreed it sounded like an enjoyable evening. I didn't mention inviting Kevin. I couldn't quite think how to work him into the mix. I had three days to figure that one out.

The next day, the sun came out and the temperature rose above freezing. Traffic was beginning to move and schools had already announced they would be in session the next day. Lane called that evening to let us know she would be in Tulsa the following week for a training session.

"I thought I would drive up Friday and spend the weekend with you two." We told her about the dinner party and she agreed it would be a fun evening.

"I've also invited Kevin Crank to join us." Peter gave me an odd look. "He was out for his run when I was getting the mail. He mentioned how glad he was to get out of the house. It just seemed like a nice thing to do." I avoided making eye contact with Peter.

"Sounds good. I enjoyed talking to him at the Epiphany Party." We talked a few more minutes before saying our good byes.

"Ev, are you playing matchmaker?" Peter asked after we had ended our call with Lane.

"Absolutely not!"

Chapter 18

I made sure all of my guests understood this was to be a casual evening. If I was going to be engaging in espionage, I certainly was not spending the day in the kitchen cooking as well! Fortunately, I had a lasagna in the freezer. The recipe was one my mother had acquired during our time in Italy. A family favorite, it never failed to get rave reviews. Jean immediately offered to bring a dessert.

I could tell Cynthia was pleased with the invitation, especially when I mentioned Jean and Randall would be joining us. I sensed she had always been a tad bit envious of the close relationship the four of us shared. In so many ways we never get out of junior high, always trying to fit into one crowd or another. I accepted Cynthia's offer to bring a salad. I could add some cheese and crackers as appetizers, a loaf of crusty bread and we had a dinner! With the addition of some wine, this would be a perfect menu for an evening of subtle interrogation.

Lane arrived shortly before our guests, giving us little time to chat. No sooner had Lane dropped her luggage in her room than the doorbell rang.

"Lane, honey, would you get the door? I need to check on the lasagna," I asked as I hurried into the kitchen.

I recognized Kevin's voice as he returned Lane's hello and

expressed surprise at realizing she was part of the evening. The two of them walked into the kitchen, Kevin holding a bottle of wine in each hand. I guess he also thought a little lubrication might help loosen a few lips this evening. Peter joined us as the doorbell rang again.

The evening's atmosphere felt relaxed and friendly. In fact, to anyone looking in, we looked like four couples enjoying a relaxing evening of good wine, food and conversation. I wasn't sure how this would aid in the investigation to unearth a Russian Sleeper Cell.

I invited the guests to settle in the dining room while I dished up the lasagna in the kitchen. Unfortunately, the dish could be as messy as it was delicious! Kevin jovially offered to take on the role of waiter, ferrying plates back and forth. 'How considerate' I thought to myself. During one of his trips he quietly ordered, "During dinner, ask Cynthia about her aunt in St. Louis." Immediately the warm thoughts I'd been having were replaced with the cold realization everything around me was part of an act. Without waiting for my response, he turned on his heel, walked into the dining room and jovially said, "This smells delicious!"

As a rule, I am quite critical of my cooking and assume people are just offering obligatory praise when eating something I've made. However, this time I had to agree with them. I know most people have a favorite version of lasagna, but I knew mom's version could go toe to toe with any of them. I waited until everyone had enjoyed a few bites of the savory pasta dish and the initial compliments had been shared. During a lull in the conversation, I turned to Cynthia and asked, "How is your aunt in St. Louis doing?" Kevin had stressed I needed to include St. Louis in my query.

"This type of recovery just takes time. Physically she is doing better, but her spirits seem to be low. I'll probably make another trip in the next few weeks."

"Are you from St. Louis?" Kevin chimed in.

"I grew up in the suburbs," Cynthia offered.

"So did I." I was beginning to see where Kevin was going with this. "Which suburb?"

I felt like there was a slight hesitation as Cynthia responded, "Kirkwood." Through lowered eyelashes, I watched Victor's demeanor throughout this interaction. That was my own idea, thank you very much.

"You're kidding! I grew up in Valley Park. But you know how all of the suburbs just run together. There was a drug store with an old-fashioned soda fountain on Kirkwood's Main Street. My grandfather used to take me there all the time."

"I know the place, but I can't remember the name. Great root beer floats," Cynthia responded. "I haven't lived there since I graduated from high school. My aunt is the only family still in the area." Victor never looked up from his plate during this interaction. I wasn't sure if Kevin had learned anything from what seemed like a pretty benign conversation.

During dessert conversation turned to travel. "I don't know if I have ever been at a table with so many well-traveled people," Kevin noted. As the group began to share their travel resumes, Peter suggested documenting how many countries the group had collectively visited. A small contingency including Peter, Kevin, Lane, Randall and Cynthia moved to the den to our map of the world. Victor and Jean stayed behind to help me clear the table.

It wasn't often I found myself in conversation with Victor Anderson. Since I obviously was not in his league academically, I figured I better stick to social norms. "I did not know Cynthia was from St. Louis until recently. Where did you grow up?" Victor is a man of few words. I figured the less I used the better.

"I'm Canadian by birth. Went to college at the University of Buffalo and filed for citizenship after I had finished my doctorate at the University of Minnesota." With that he laid plates near the sink and headed to join the group in the den.

"Victor is not much for small talk, is he?" Jean asked as she came up alongside me.

"No." Left a little stunned by his sudden departure, I made a mental note to report to Kevin how rehearsed and abrupt his answer had been.

"I believe Kevin is smitten with our Lane," Jean said with a sly smile.

Talk about a change of direction, "What?" Even I knew I responded too quickly and loudly.

"I assumed that was part of your plan tonight. Create a social situation that puts the two of them together. I don't mind being part of the ruse."

"Actually, I had already invited Kevin. Lane called at the last minute to let us know she was coming to town. No subterfuge on my part."

"Well, I definitely sensed some interest on both of their parts," Jean said thoughtfully.

Had I been so involved in my role as an FBI Asset trying to uncover a plot to destroy democracy and thwart off a potential global pandemic that I had missed sparks between my daughter and Kevin?

By the time Jean and I joined the group, approximately thirty-five pins marked countries visited by someone in attendance. In fact, the only continent not visited was Antarctica.

"Which countries are included in the Hanser Center's program?" asked Kevin. He might be doing this unintentionally, but Kevin was certainly ingratiating himself to Peter. A new set of pins with different colored heads, was retrieved. Peter and Randall began marking these locations. As the group focused on the map, I took the opportunity to watch my daughter. She seemed pretty keen on Kevin as well. Whether by design or accident the two of them stood side by side, joking and laughing as the map began to fill with more pins.

As the evening drew on, each individual was assigned a pin color and ordered to mark the map with their travels. Although no one intended for it to become a competition, that is definitely where it seemed to be headed.

In the end, Randall nosed out Peter by two countries. I came in next on the list followed by Jean and then Lane. The Andersons were a distant sixth and Kevin was dead last with only two countries marked.

"Guess I have some catching up to do! I've got to get a picture of this. It's inspirational." Kevin said jovially as he snapped a photo with his phone.

The group moved to the living room and settled into the overstuffed couches and chairs. I was quite aware Lane and Kevin had ended up side by side.

Once seated, Kevin turned to Victor and asked, "So explain to me a little more about the DARPA Center. I heard a reference to DARPA on NPR this morning and it made me curious to learn more."

"A Defense Advanced Research Project Agency (DARPA) grant is a collection of scientists with a particular set of skills. A type of think tank. The grant creates a center that is tasked with solving a particular type of problem specifically related to defense."

"It sounds like a big deal to receive one of these grants," Kevin said encouragingly. "What is your center's project?"

"The goal of the program is to develop bio-surveillance technology to detect pathogens before they become a threat. This can have huge ramifications for the military as well as the general public,"

Victor's voice was laced with pride.

Randall chimed in. "Victor has worked quite strategically to line up just the right collection of scientists to make DFU a viable option. Well done, Victor," Randall said as he raised his glass to toast Victor.

I directed my gaze towards Cynthia as we all toasted Victor. She was definitely smiling but there was something about her demeanor that felt off. Did I detect a flicker of jealousy?

The party broke up around 10:00 pm, with everyone but Kevin leaving. Apparently at some point he and Lane had discussed movies and found they shared a love of *The Princess Bride*. As Peter and I said our good nights, the two of them settled onto the couch with a bowl of popcorn and queued up the movie.

Peter fell asleep almost immediately. Which inexplicably irritated the heck out of me. True he knew nothing of my current double life and the concerns I had regarding Lane's potential interest in an undercover FBI agent. As sleep eluded me, I laid in bed listening to the distant sounds of the movie and their laughter. I really wasn't sure how I felt about this turn of events. Was Kevin just using Lane as a cover? Was she attracted to him? Where could this lead? Tonight, it wasn't just night sweats keeping me awake. Throughout the night I threw the covers off and then would pull them back on, tossing and turning. At one point, Peter rolled over and threw his arm across my stomach. I pushed it off and turned on my side, not sure if he was reading something into my fitful state. But as I've told him before, at this stage in my life, throwing off the covers and disrobing does not mean what it once did!

 I would definitely be having a conversation with Kevin about his intentions with my daughter at our next meeting.

Chapter 19

I was enjoying my second cup of coffee when Lane emerged from her bedroom. Since my eyes opened this morning, I'd been rehearsing different conversations in my mind that would ask, without prying, about her evening with Kevin. Past experience told me; I should not lead with an inquisition. I would have to work it naturally into the conversation. After all, I was currently working in the espionage field. If I could be part of exposing Russian spies, surely, I could glean information from my own daughter.

"So, dad said you're headed for Greece this summer," Lane commented as she sipped her coffee. "I need to check my work calendar, but I'm hoping I can meet up with you."

"Excellent! Dad just ran out to the store, but when he gets home, we can get a calendar and solidify some dates." The only thing better than traveling with Peter was when Lane joined us.

"Kevin and I are going to grab a cup of coffee later, otherwise I'm totally free today to talk travel." I wasn't sure if the gleam in her eye was about the travel or Kevin, but I had just been given my opening.

"The two of you seemed to hit it off," I casually said. I learned a long time ago to use open ended statements and questions with my daughter. As close as we are, I do my best to respect her privacy.

Peter always says, "If she wants us to know something, she'll tell us." Which is true. However, sometimes you have to create a fertile environment for conversation.

"We had a good time watching the movie. I can't say we've spent much time in real conversation, but he seems like a nice guy. Maybe a little lonely. Deep Fork is a great town, but it's tough to connect with people our age, especially when you're single."

"I've had lunch and coffee with him a few times. I think you have a good read on him." Again, I was trying to leave the ball in Lane's court.

"Anyway, I suggested we get coffee and if the weather cooperates maybe take a walk." With that, Lane picked up her coffee and headed to the shower.

At lunch we enjoyed left-overs from the night before and began planning our summer trip. It looked like I would meet Peter in Istanbul the last week of June and together we would travel to Greece for a three-week holiday. If work allowed, Lane would arrive the second week of July.

After much discussion, we decided to stay on Mykonos Island this trip. There is a reason it is so popular with tourists. Its picturesque Cycladic architecture, the narrow streets of Chora, beautiful beaches and oh the sunsets. Although not a priority for Peter and me, Mykonos does boast an exciting nightlife. Mindful that traveling with your parents may not always be the most exciting option, we agreed it would be nice for Lane to at least have the opportunity to spend a night on the town.

Thanks to online resources, we found a beautiful vacation rental with a distant view of the Aegean Sea. Since this wasn't our first trip to Greece, we all felt comfortable not being in the heart of the tourist district. Everything we would enjoy was accessible by car, ferry or scooter. We would have ample time to navigate the sights we wanted to visit as well as soak up some of the Mediterranean culture and sun. I found myself wondering if I would need to request time off from my spying gig.

The three of us were immersed in planning our trip when the doorbell rang. Lane jumped up, "Oh my gosh it's 3:00! Mom could you get the door? I need to run to the bathroom."

It may have been my imagination, but I thought Kevin looked a bit sheepish as I opened the door. "Hi, Evelyn. Thank you for last night. The lasagna was delicious and the company very interesting. I appreciate being included," he said as Peter walked up behind me.

"Kevin, we've been planning a trip to Greece. Let me show you our skeleton itinerary," Peter chirped as he led Kevin to the dining room table. "After I finish the trip with students, Ev will join me in Istanbul, and then we'll go to Greece. Lane will join us at some point as well."

Both men were immersed in the computer when Lane emerged from her bedroom. I noted she had freshened her makeup and changed tops. My mom radar told me she saw this as more than just a coffee between acquaintances. Once again, I made a mental note to visit with Kevin about this development. I might be complicit in helping to save the free world, but I would not let my daughter be used or possibly hurt.

That evening, we had tickets to a concert at the Carnegie Cultural Arts Center. Like many downtowns in the 1980's, Deep Fork saw a lot of vacant buildings as well as a decaying Carnegie library. The city and DFU partnered to renovate and add on to the original library to create a performing arts center which served both the community and the university. As a result of this partnership, a broad spectrum of cultural opportunities was provided for both students and the community. This evening's performance was a string quartet. We were able to secure a last minute third ticket so Lane could join us.

I anticipated seeing the entire Jung family at the concert and was not disappointed. Jin and Min valued cultural experiences for their sons and took advantage of everything the performing arts center provided. Since both boys took violin lessons, I was doubly certain they would be attending this evening's performance.

During intermission, we located the Jungs in the crowd. Sam and Mee were politely sipping lemonade and munching on cookies. As often was the case when I saw a boy of any age, my thoughts turned to Bobby, wondering what he would look like at that age or what his interests would be.

"Are you enjoying the concert?" Min politely asked.

Her question broke my reminiscent mood and drew me back to the present. Remembering my assignment to find out about any travel plans they had, I broached the subject of summer vacation.

"Peter, Lane and I spent the day planning a summer trip to Greece. It's been such a gray winter; I'm looking forward to some sun. Do you all have any trips on the horizon?" I asked in my best conversational tone.

"I'll be taking the boys to visit my parents in Michigan this summer," Min stated. "It's always nice to get out of the Oklahoma heat."

"I'm sure the boys enjoy spending time with their grandparents. How old were you when your parents left South Korea?" Although I knew the answer, I wanted to use it as a springboard for my next question.

"I was born in Michigan, I'm a first generation American," Min said with pride.

"That's right, I had forgotten. But, Jin, you were born in South Korea, correct?" The cautious, albeit brief, look between Jin and Min spoke volumes to me.

"Yes, I was born in Seoul. I came to the United States after finishing my bachelor's degree at the University of South Korea. My parents are dead. I have no siblings." Talk about shutting down any further conversation!

Just then, we were joined by the Patels. Kamya once again wore a beautiful sari. As Lane was oohing and aahing over it, I turned to Manasi. "We were just talking about our travel plans for the summer. Will you and Kamya be traveling to India?

"Yes, my nephew in Bangalore has been quite ill. Sadly, his prognosis is not good."

"I'm so sorry to hear that," which I truly was. The pain in his eyes attributed to the truth of his statement. "Has he been ill for a while?"

"Unfortunately, yes. Ten years ago, his kidneys began failing. Although I gave him one of mine, it seems the medicine he has taken to prevent rejection is no longer successful. He started on dialysis last month. The doctors do not think he could survive another transplant. It is a very sad time for our family."

As Manasi shared this information, Kamya gently took his hand and squeezed it. The lights blinked and we were called back into the auditorium.

Throughout the rest of the evening's performance, I found myself thinking about the Patels. Kevin had intonated there might be some connection with Bratva, the Russian mafia. If Manasi's nephew was dealing with such a devastating illness, could it somehow be used into coercing Manasi into feeding information to the Russians. Although I didn't see how, I knew it wasn't my job to judge what information was relevant and what was not. I definitely would be sharing this newly acquired news with Kevin.

As had become my routine, I waited for Peter's gentle snoring before I retrieved the burner phone from my sock drawer.

Succinctly, I sent Kevin the information I had gleaned from the evening's conversations. I received an immediate acknowledgement as well as a summons to meet sometime the next day. I let Kevin know I would not be available until Lane had left for Tulsa. More than likely, later in the afternoon. "Understood" was the response I received.

Chapter 20

My soul feels the fullest when Peter, Lane and I attend church together. The words of grace and hope, up-lifting music and fellowship of a faith family are a cornerstone of my life. In times of darkness and chaos, my faith has provided the anchor needed to ride out the storm. I have come to deeply value the wisdom people of every generation have in living out their faith. This morning the Benson family sat in front of us. Emma and Hannah were as good as anyone could expect a five and three-year-old to behave. However, there was constant twitching, whispering and craning of necks throughout the service as they worked their way through the busy bag Lauren had brought for each girl. Yet, just before the last song, three-year-old Hannah said to no one in particular, "Jesus loves me, this I know." Way to cut to the heart of it Hannah, I thought.

Sunday finally offered a break from the gray weather we had experienced for the past few weeks, bringing a sunny, crisp day. Lane and I took a long walk, accessing the downtown via the neighborhood's pedestrian bridge and then circled back through the neighborhood. We weren't the only ones enjoying the beautiful day. As we made our way through the neighborhood, we chatted with a variety of neighbors also taking advantage of the respite from winter. Turning the corner, we came face to face with Miss Essie dressed in a fuschia colored velour jogging suit with a sock monkey knit cap doing her own version of speed walking.

"It's a beautiful day for a walk," I offered as she moved past us.

Without breaking stride, the octogenarian responded, "If you rest, you rust."

Before going home, we made a point of stopping in to see Jo Walker. Since 'the general's' death, Jo had either been in Oklahoma City or had one of her daughter's staying with her. This would be her first night alone since Bill's death.

I could see the exhaustion in Jo's face as soon as she answered the door. We accepted her offer to come in, but I made a mental note to keep the visit short. Normally, Jo would have peppered Lane with questions about her career and love life. Today the questions were brief and half-hearted.

We were beginning to make signs of leaving when Jo turned to me and said, "I've been going through Bill's things and found his journal. You know Bill, he was always patrolling the neighborhood. What most people don't know is that he kept notes. I suppose it might have been offensive to some of our neighbors, but that was never his intent. It just seems a shame to get rid of it. Since you and Peter have been in the neighborhood as long as anyone else, I thought you might want to have it. You know, keep up Bill's work."

I could sense the mental eyeroll Lane must be doing as I graciously accepted the notebook. A few weeks ago, I might have had the same reaction. But now, in my role as an FBI Asset, I saw it as a possible source of serendipitous intelligence. As soon as we entered our house, Lane announced to her dad he was being charged as the new 'general' of the neighborhood.

Around 4:00 pm Lane packed up her car and headed to Tulsa for her training. It sounded like we might be fortunate enough to see her at the end of the week as well. Peter announced he was going in to the office to get a jump on the week, leaving me with a few hours to myself. Normally, I would have curled up on the couch with a good book. But leading a double life does not allow for such luxuries. I texted Kevin I was available. We arranged to meet in the Walmart parking lot.

I arrived at the designated parking lot approximately thirty minutes later and pulled in next to Kevin's car. He signaled for me to climb into the passenger's side where I found a ballcap and sunglasses. "This should be enough of a disguise for today." With that, he pulled out of the parking lot and we began our meeting.

"I'll be recording today's conversation for later reference. Let's start with the Patels. Can you elaborate on their relative you mentioned?"

"Apparently, ten years ago Manasi donated a kidney to his nephew who lives in India. I've been racking my brain trying to remember if I knew this. I have to say, I don't think it was ever mentioned. The Patels are often gone for months at a time, both visiting family and with his international work. However, that also seems to be about the time they were on a yearlong sabbatical. I'm assuming that is probably when the transplant happened. As I recall, it was during his sabbatical he served as interim director of Global Health Biotech." I was working hard to reconstruct the timeline and itineraries of Patel's travels over the past twenty years.

"I'll double check the timing with our database. According to my dossier, he was the director, not interim director," Kevin noted.

"That's true. He served as director prior to joining the DFU faculty. But, over the years he has, more than once, held an interim position as they transitioned directors. I said he was on sabbatical, but actually, now that I think about it, I believe he took a year's leave of absence to accept the interim position."

"Can you give me a read on their attitude and emotions as they told you about their nephew's illness?" Kevin queried.

"They were both genuinely sad."

"So, you sense they were telling the truth?" Kevin's questioned.

I was taken aback as I contemplated what I had observed the evening before might be a fabricated story. I mulled this possibility over for a few minutes before responding.

"Yes, I believe they were telling the truth. If you had seen the deep sorrow in both Kamya and Manasi's eyes you would have no doubt of their sincerity. There was a true tenderness between the two of them, the type forged by a shared grief."

Sensing this exchange had dredged up memories of my own heartache, Kevin waited a few minutes before he continued on with his agenda.

"Let's move on to the Jungs. We've verified Min's parent's location and their immigration to the USA several years before she was born. Have you gathered any information concerning Jin?

I found myself choosing my words quite carefully as I relayed my observations to Kevin. "When I asked about his family, his answer was quite specific and felt rehearsed. I sensed it was designed to head off any further questioning. He emphasized his parents were dead and he had no siblings, plus I sensed a nervousness from Min during our conversation. Have you been able to find out anything more from his background?"

"Jin's defection from North Korea coincides with the end of his military service. There are a few seemingly unrelated incidences that place him in the vicinity of a hit and run. His defection happened two weeks after the accident."

"Do you think he defected to avoid being charged?" I was shocked to think Jin would have avoided taking responsibility for something that serious.

"That is definitely one scenario. Another is that he was framed for the accident. That type of leverage would have allowed the government to coerce him into working for them either legitimately or as a spy. Either way their reaction to the break in at their house makes sense. They're living in fear of being found out. The question is, what are they hiding?"

We drove in silence for a few minutes, allowing me to absorb this new information.

"I want to spend a few minutes de-briefing from last Friday's dinner party. Your guests have an impressive travel record. I sent the picture I took of the travel board to the Bureau. They're in the process of relaying the information through our data bases seeing if we can find any discrepancies. Being a weekend, it is taking a little longer than I would hope." I definitely picked up on an undertone of frustration on his part.

"I didn't know spies got the weekend off," I jokingly offered.

"Technically, we are not spies," he corrected me. "And, a great portion of the Bureau's tech geeks are nine to fivers. There is a contingency that monitors high risk, immediate threats, but our case does not fall into that category. Ours is a long game."

He continued, "I was a little surprised the Andersons' list of travel was comparatively short. Tell me more about them."

"Victor is brilliant and can be stand-offish. I was a little surprised at their travel resume as well. Generally, faculty involved in research tend to confer with colleagues around the world, which obviously can lead to extensive travel. As Vice President of Research, I would have expected his passport to have more stamps."

"See what you can do to find out about his limited travel. Tell me about Cynthia."

"As you know, she works in Randall's office with finances. She is definitely the social butterfly of the couple. Always at events, comes early and stays late. She is also a joiner. I can think of at least four groups she is actively involved in. As a rule, you can expect Victor to be at home and Cynthia to be out and about. She's great to have at a party. She can make conversation with anyone and often gets the most reserved person to open up." I was finding as I described my neighbors in this context, many of their behaviors began to become suspect. "It's funny, as I'm describing Cynthia, I realize I know very little about her."

"What organizations is she involved in?"

"Although she is not faculty, she has served as the staff representative to the faculty council for several years. This organization serves as the faculty voice when dealing with administrative issues. There seems to be a lot of politics with this group. She also belongs to a women's university leadership council. Although it originally was designed to offer mentorship to women joining the faculty, my sense is that it has become more of an organization that strokes each other's egos. A group she and Victor are both active in is a Supper Club for Scientists. The group was a spin-off from the community's Newcomers Club. However, this particular group went rogue a few years back and became very specific in the type of people included. Kind of defeated the purpose in meeting a broad spectrum of folks in the community. It really is a Who's Who of DFU research. Lastly, she is active in Deep Fork's Service League. Again, somewhat the upper echelon of our community. They definitely do a lot of good work, but the members are all of a certain socio-economic status. "

"She's strategically placed herself to associate with a specific type of people," Kevin observed.

"As nice as she is, I've always thought of Cynthia as a bit of a social climber, perhaps needing to validate her own worth. In fact, the other night as you were praising Victor's accomplishments in securing the DARPA Center, I was watching Cynthia. I definitely sensed a bit of jealousy, perhaps even resentment on her part. It was fleeting, but definitely there," I contemplated.

"Your observation skills were one of the reasons we recruited you," Kevin shared.

"That and I outed you," I said with a grin.

"Well, there was that. But you have good instincts. Much of what you have shared with me is what you observed by watching people's reactions to what is going on around them. Most of us, when we are 'on', can play a role. It's when you're the secondary player that our expressions and body language tell volumes about what we are really thinking."

With that, he turned the topic on a dime. "We're still following the thread connecting the Webers to the families in Turkey. What we've discovered is one of the families referred to in your story does, in fact, have ties to the Russian mob Bratva."

"Wait! Isn't that the same group you suspect may have ties to the Patels?" My head was beginning to hurt.

"We have not verified a connection between Bratva and either couple, but it is unsettling that there seems to be the possibility of influence with multiple couples," he cautioned.

We drove quietly for a few moments as I internalized the information I had received today. I was so lost in thought that I completely forgot about 'the general's' notebook until I reached for a cough drop and felt its presence in my purse.

As I handed the notebook to Kevin, I explained how it came to be in my guardianship. "I have not looked through the book so I have no idea if there is anything valuable or not." Although I didn't tell Kevin, the real reason I had not perused the contents is that I did not want to find anything negative that might have been written about Peter and me. I preferred to keep my memories of 'the general' as fond as possible.

"I'll begin an analysis of its contents this evening. Looks like our time is up." As he pulled into the Walmart parking lot, he gestured to the back seat. "These sacks are for you. In case Peter's home when you return, you had better be holding some bags." I noted toilet paper, toothpaste, tea as well as a few other things were props in my cover story. The FBI is really quite thorough!

"There is one more thing we need to discuss, Lane." Before I exited the car, I intended to get some clarity regarding his relationship with my daughter.

Kevin took his hand off the steering wheel and slowly turned to me, "Yes."

"To use a cliché, *what are your intentions with my daughter?*"

I could tell he was carefully framing his answer to my question. "Lane is an exceptional young woman. She's intelligent, funny and very sensitive to others. Like you, she can read people very well. Sensing a single man my age might lack a social life in Deep Fork, she offered a little companionship while she is in town. I have simply responded to her kindness."

Making sure I had full eye contact, I emphatically stated, "I will not have my daughter hurt. If I feel she is being used in any way, our relationship is terminated."

Matching my gaze, he affirmed, "Understood."

Chapter 21

A few days later, I woke to a text indicating there had been a breakthrough in the Jungs' surveillance. Kevin asked if I had an opportunity to meet later in the day. I texted back I'd be available after class. Still enjoying an unseasonably warm winter day, I indicated I would take a midafternoon walk along the creek path. This would give me access to Kevin's back door without the concern of being seen by neighbors.

Curiosity about Kevin's news was simmering on my brain's back burner as my class enjoyed a vigorous discussion concerning the treatment of the Osage tribe during the oil boom of the 1920's. I was both delighted at my students' outrage over the atrocities that occurred and exhausted from the intensity of the dialogue. A walk seemed like a great way to unwind, even if it was going to end with a covert meeting.

Painfully aware my once safe neighborhood had been compromised, I slipped the can of pepper spray Kevin had given me into my pocket. Cutting through the Webers' side yard, I picked up the creek path. The winter sunlight filtered through the trees as I took in deep breaths of air. Although I would have enjoyed a much longer walk, I turned off the path and worked my way to Kevin's back door. The evergreen trees provided enough cover that I would not be spotted from any of the nearby homes.

Kevin greeted me at the back door and immediately offered me a beverage. *He's becoming one of us,* I thought to myself as I accepted a glass of water.

Entering the command post, I noticed additional notes had been added to the evidence board. The Jungs' section had multiple notations, obviously the reason for today's meeting.

"We've picked up a conversation between Min and Jin concerning the time between the hit and run and Jin's defection. From the intelligence we've gathered, Jin was in the car, but not driving. Strong-arming citizens into complying with their political agenda is a hallmark of North Korea's government. It appears the accident was staged to frame Jin and coerce him into joining a team developing a nuclear bomb. At an early age Jin had been targeted by the North Koreans as a brilliant mind who could potentially help propel them into the nuclear age," Kevin updated me.

"But his field is molecular biology," I noted.

"Yes, once he defected, he shifted his focus. He spoke the truth when he said he was an only child. However, at the time of his defection both parents were still alive. Apparently, he has had no interaction with them since he left, both for their protection and his. My guess is he was already planning to defect when they framed him for the hit and run. He bought a new identity, changed his career path and created a new life. The long and short of the conversations we've intercepted dealt with his constant fear of being found out. The break-in was a huge trigger. Although he has had no direct contact with his parents, he has been able to keep track of them through some distant relatives. His father passed away last year. Jin has felt compelled to keep closer tabs on his mother since then. Their fear is this increased contact has brought them to the attention of the North Korean government. As best we can tell, this isn't the case," Kevin continued.

"What about the attack on Min at the research center?"

"Unrelated to the North Korea situation, but still linked to our investigation. Unfortunately, Min was in the wrong place at the wrong time. Of course, it has added to their paranoia."

"So, the Jungs are cleared?" I could hear the relief in my voice.

"Yes. Would you like to do the honors?" he asked as he held up the red marker. Drawing a red X through their names and pictures did give me satisfaction but at the same time made me painfully aware of the faces still staring back at me.

"What happens with the Jungs now?" I queried.

"Nothing, as far as the Bureau is concerned."

"It must have been incredibly hard for his parents to say goodbye to their only child." My mother's heart hurt for Jin's parents. There are many ways to lose a child, I thought to myself. "Is there any way Min's mother could be brought to the United States?" I asked hopefully.

"Again, Evelyn, this is not a problem for the FBI." Kevin emphatically stated.

"But still, it would be a humane gesture," I coaxed.

"Politics is rarely about doing the humane thing," Kevin said grimly.

Understanding this was a battle I could not win; I made a mental note to extend additional kindness to the Jung family. "So now there are three," I noted as I turned towards the evidence board.

"Yes. I've had the Bureau running travel and passport information on all three couples. In the cases of the Webers and Andersons, I want to verify their list of countries visited concurs with the State Department's database." Kevin continued, "As I mentioned earlier, I'm surprised at the Andersons' lack of international travel. According to the information I gathered the other night, Victor has been to Canada, England, Austria, Germany and Italy. Cynthia has been to all of the same countries except for Austria."

"They are not a couple who vacations internationally. Really, they don't travel a whole lot, unless it is related to business," I mused. "Often times, they travel separately, Cynthia mainly to St. Louis and Victor when it is related to the university. In the twelve years they've lived behind us, I probably have only had to check on their house a half dozen times. Even then, it has just been to water outside plants. The only time I can recall checking on the inside was after a storm when we had a power outage. I wanted to make sure their refrigerated food was all right. Come to think of it, I thought Cynthia was a bit irritated I had done that," I paused, rolling that revelation over in my mind. "Why would she give me a key if she didn't want me to have access to her house?"

"If they're spies, they would want to fit into the culture of the neighborhood. Giving you a key but never asking you to check on things inside would support their identity yet protect their privacy. At this point we don't have any evidence to support any suspicions, but it's worth noting." With that he added a post-it briefly describing the power outage incident.

"Have you had a chance to read the general's notebooks?" I asked.

"I'm slowly filtering through and sorting out any pertinent information," Kevin shared. "By the way, there is nothing unkind about you and Peter. Any references made about the two of you were always positive. I would say he was quite fond of both of you."

I had to look away as tears welled up in my eyes. Although the big picture of what we were doing had implications for national security, at the end of the day, someone who was loved had been murdered. For the first time since this whole adventure had started, I felt anger welling up inside of me. Someone on that board not only was a spy but also a murderer. With new resolve, I internally vowed to do what I could to find 'the general's' murderer.

"On another note, I received a text from Lane last night," Kevin cautiously said. "She'll be back in town this weekend and offered to put together a gathering of her local friends. Introduce me to some people nearer my age." I could tell he was avoiding eye contact as he shared this bit of information. "I wanted to run it by you before I responded."

Peter and I recently watched a movie where a mother orchestrated opportunities for her daughter to meet certain eligible bachelors. Needless to say, the whole thing backfired, but in the end love triumphed. At the end, Peter clicked the television off with the remote and said, "Well, there are two hours of my life I'll never get back," and went to bed. I'm a sucker for sappy movies, especially when I know it ends with everyone living happily ever after. Which brings me to the present. Do I want to be the mother who dictates who my daughter spends time with? Well, if I'm totally honest, yes. My happiness parallels Lane's. However, I also respected her ability to make wise and careful choices.

"Under normal circumstances, would you take advantage of an offer like the one Lane made?" I asked, making sure to maintain eye contact during my interrogation.

"Yes, I would."

"Do you see this get-together as part of your cover story?"

"It does serve that purpose."

"Are you interested in my daughter beyond her role as a way to connect you to others in town?" I held my breath anticipating his answer.

"I have learned to put my personal feelings aside while undercover."

"That does not really answer my question."

"It's the best I can offer at this time," Kevin honestly answered.

During dinner, both Peter's and my phone dinged indicating we had received a text. Checking the message, Peter smiled. "Lane is coming through this weekend. Should be here late Friday evening. Apparently, she's put together a gathering of some of her local friends at Amore for Saturday evening. Interesting, she's included Kevin." I remained silent as I took a sip of wine. "What does your 'mom radar' tell you about this one, Ev? Do you think there is a spark between Lane and Kevin?"

"Time will tell."

Chapter 22

"Dmitry is coming to visit!" Peter announced cheerfully the following morning. "I just received an e-mail last night. He will be in the states for business and plans to swing by here the middle of next week."

"This is a surprise," I truthfully said. Ironic, the man who had put Peter and me at the top of the FBI's Suspect List would be making his first trip to our home during an active FBI investigation. "We've never had the pleasure of hosting Dmitry. How long will he be staying?"

"I'm surprised as well. As a rule, his business keeps him on one coast or the other. He usually doesn't visit the fly-over states." Double checking his e-mail Peter confirmed the dates. "Looks like two nights, arriving on Tuesday and leaving on Thursday. Would you contact Jean to see if she and Randall are available for dinner next Wednesday?"

"I'd be happy to but I didn't realize they knew Dmitry?"

"Randall does. About five years ago, Randall joined me for the last week of the students' trip. We ended in Paris where Dmitry happened to be on a business trip. The three of us had the most excellent dinner in a little café in the Place Royale. Definitely out of an academic's price range but Dmitry insisted on buying dinner. Perhaps it was the amount of wine we consumed that night, but the two of them hit it off. I'm sure I told you about it. They've kept in touch ever since. In fact, they frequently see each other when Randall is travelling overseas."

"Sounds like an enjoyable evening. However, the fact that your last meal together was in a five-star Parisian restaurant puts a bit of pressure on me to cook an out of this world meal." Although it was said with sarcasm, I was truly intimidated. While pursuing my undercover activities, I also would need to prepare a superb meal, worthy of a Michelin guide rating!

I decided to start my morning with a brisk walk. Not only did I need the cardio exercise, but I also needed time to process the symphony of information playing through my mind. Rounding the corner, I ran into Min walking Sam and Mee to school. I immediately changed directions and joined them. The boys were everything a six and eight-year-old should be, anxious to run ahead and then stop dead in their tracks to pick up an interesting rock. Once again, the ache I often felt when watching boys play crept through my heart. But the sadness I felt today was for a grandmother who would never be able to enjoy the gift of watching her grandchildren grow up. Before I was consumed with melancholy, I turned my attention to Min.

"It's a beautiful morning. It was so gray for so long, I'm truly enjoying the sunshine," I shared.

"Yes, it is lovely," she agreed, "but, you must remember to wear sunscreen." Min was always practical and not one for small talk. However, I was determined to follow through on my vow to mindfully show increased kindness to the Jung family.

"Of course. The boys are getting so tall. Are they enjoying school?"

"They both are receiving excellent marks. Sam seems to have a propensity for math while Mee seems to be more science focused."

"Following in their parents' footsteps," I noted.

After depositing the boys, we turned and retraced our steps towards the Jung house. As we parted ways, I offered babysitting services if she and Jin wanted a date night. I noted the gratitude in her eyes as she thanked me for the offer.

Refreshed after my morning walk, I took care of a few chores around the house and gathered my gear for my yoga class. I was feeling quite proud of my fitness-focused morning as I entered the yoga studio. Jean waved me over to join her, Cynthia and Kamya. Smiling at me were three of the same faces that occupied the FBI's evidence board of suspected Russian spies. The knot that had resided in my stomach since I discovered my house was bugged, tightened as I greeted the ladies.

Some days are better than others in my yoga practice. This was not a stellar day. As the class moved into tree pose, I could not achieve the focus I needed to maintain balance. My thoughts and eyes kept turning towards the three women surrounding me. What would be the tipping point? When would there be clarity as to which of these ladies were complicit in an espionage plot and potentially a murderer? As we ended our practice in Savasana, the relaxation I normally felt eluded me. Sensing someone nearby, I fluttered my eyes open to see my yoga instructor staring over me. "Evelyn, you're quite unfocused and tense today. Let me rub a little lavender oil over your temples." With that, she knelt down and gently massaged my temples and jaws. As her hands glided over my face, I could feel my facial muscles begin to ease. Unfortunately, relaxation eluded the rest of my body as our session came to an end.

While rolling up our mats, I turned to Jean and inquired about their availability for dinner the following week with Dmitry.

"I'm excited to meet the great Dmitry! As Randall describes him, he seems like a larger than life character," Jean enthusiastically stated. "I'll double check our schedule tonight."

The Neighborhood

As we joined Cynthia and Kamya, I decided to seize the opportunity to have the "gang of three" together and proposed we enjoy an early lunch. All agreed, so we threw our mats in our respective cars and walked the block and a half to Two Brothers.

After placing our orders, we chit chatted for a few minutes before I asked, "Has anyone visited with Jo lately?" I was hoping one of them would break under my intense interrogation and cop to having murdered 'the general'. Instead, I was rewarded with clucking of sympathetic neighbors.

"Yesterday, I invited Jo for tea. We had a lovely visit," Kamya gently shared. "Such sadness. Losing a loved one is difficult no matter the age..." her voice trailed off as she became lost in her own thoughts.

"I stopped by for a visit as well," Cynthia chimed in. "We spent over an hour sharing memories about 'the general' and his patrol of the neighborhood. Of course, I was sensitive enough not to call him that in front of Jo. However, she was well aware of his reputation. Did you know he kept a log of his walks and things he saw? Evelyn, she said you have the book now."

Instinctively, I realized I needed to be careful how I answered this query. "She did give it to me when Lane and I stopped by last week. It was all Lane could do to keep from rolling her eyes. As soon as we got home, she told Peter about the book and said he could become the new general."

Giggling, Jean said, "I can just imagine Peter on an evening patrol. At the very least he would increase everyone's IQ on the architecture of their house. So, fill us in, what types of things did 'the general' record?"

Three weeks ago, I would have taken this as an innocent query. But those days were behind me. "Honestly, I have not opened it and really have no desire to. I believe the notebook will just gather dust in a closet."

I wasn't sure, but thought I had just given information that might force the guilty party to take action. At the very least, their concern about being found out might be heightened. If 'the general' knew something incriminating, it was more than likely in the notebook. My list of things to tell Kevin was growing.

After lunch, I ran home, showered, changed and drove to my office to begin the grading process. The first paper of the semester had been turned in by the students. My thoroughness in responding to their work on this first paper sets the tone for the semester. I pepper the margins with questions, comments and suggestions of how they might improve the articulation of their thoughts. Ultimately, the comments I make are what will truly benefit the students' academic growth, not the grade. I'm not sure they see it that way, but I certainly do. Daylight was fading as I took off my glasses and rubbed my tired eyes.

"How goes it?" Peter was standing in my office door wearing a smile. I feel so blessed to have someone in my life who greets me at the beginning and end of the day with a smile. Briefly, my mind turned to Jo and the emptiness she must now be feeling. "Better, now that you are here. Let's go get some dinner."

I laid in bed waiting for the tell-tale sign Peter was asleep, snoring. Once I was sure he was out for the night, I retrieved the burner phone and sent Kevin an update.

Dmitry Sergey will be visiting next week. He is in the states for a business trip and is coming through for a brief visit. Peter asked to invite Randall and Jean for dinner when he is here. They met several years ago and hit it off.

Lunched with Cynthia, Jean and Kamya today. Jo Weber had told Cynthia about the notebook. I indicated it was gathering dust in a closet in my house.

Kevin must have been anticipating my text, because I received a quick response:

How often does Dmitry visit you?

He has never been to our home.

May I install surveillance cameras outside of your house? We may catch someone looking for the notebook.

Not sure how you'll do that without raising suspicion.

I have my ways.

The next morning, we awoke to find our cable service was not working. I assured Peter I would take care of it. Once he left, I followed up on last night's text chain:

Are you responsible for our cable outage?

A repairman will be there this afternoon to take care of everything.

Debbie Williams

Chapter 23

By the time Friday evening rolled around, the three of us were exhausted. Lane's training had focused on the intricate and technical components of web-based travel services. Peter was deep in the throes of planning the summer abroad trip. Although he had a competent staff, it was still a time-intensive process making sure all the moving pieces evolved into a cohesive travel experience. I had finished grading the last paper the previous evening and returned them to the students during today's class. Over the years I'd made it a practice to offer special office hours after the return of the first round of papers. Although time-consuming, it was appreciated by many of the students, especially those who received a mark lower than they had expected. As usual, the sign-up sheet I'd offered at the end of class for thirty-minute consultations filled up quickly. I finished the last consultation at 4:30 pm with a high-achieving biology major who rarely received a grade below an A. The average mark she received on her paper had sent her into a minor tailspin. Once again, my lay ministry training on active listening came in handy. I let the agitated young lady spend the first ten minutes of our session sharing her frustrations as I reflected back the feelings she was emanating. Ultimately, I turned the angst expressed into a positive "what can we learn from this paper and experience." As a rule, this is the first time most students see past the grade and turn their focus to the comments and suggestions written on their paper. At the end of our session, the young lady seemed in a better state, resolved to follow the suggestions I had made on her next paper. After a half dozen such meetings, I was physically and emotionally exhausted.

A long-standing tradition in the Johns' household after a stressful week is no-cooking, no clean-up Friday. Which was the reason we were enjoying Chinese takeout. Conversation was uncharacteristically limited as we finished off the last of the cashew chicken. Afterwards, Peter started a fire and we each took our respective seats on the living room furniture. Snuggled under throws with pillows strategically placed, Lane and I turned on a chick flick while Peter buried his nose in a book. It was exactly the kind of evening I cherished, the three of us contentedly spending time together. Not wanting to upset the serenity of the evening, I had purposely not quizzed Lane about her Saturday evening plans with Kevin and friends.

By the time Lane sauntered out of her room the next morning, I was sitting at the dining room table surrounded by cookbooks. Normally, I don't overthink and stress about meals I'm preparing for company. However, the whole international espionage situation, coupled with memories of an exquisite French dinner, had me a little on edge. I even did an internet search for appropriate meals to serve spies. Unfortunately, this only led me to spy themed birthday parties for kids. I did not think having juice boxes as a beverage option would be appreciated. After skimming through several cookbooks, I landed on Julia Child's Beef Bourguignon recipe.

Lane looked over my shoulder at the menu I had scribbled onto a pad of paper. Next to the word dessert was a question mark. "I'd go with something easy," was Lane's wise advice. Knowing the stew would take all day and every pan I owned, I had to agree that would be the smart move.

"Remember that ice cream dish we had at the French restaurant in Dallas?" She asked. "It was so simple. Just a scoop of vanilla ice cream topped with Amaretto liqueur and fresh coffee grounds. It was really delicious," she shared. Bingo! I had my dessert.

As I closed my recipe books, I casually asked if she had ironed out the details for the evening's plans. Out of the corner of my eye, I could see her back stiffen as she finished pouring a cup of coffee. "Mom, I'm just extending some kindness to someone who seems a little lonely. Something I learned from my mother; I think." I decided to take that as a compliment but intended to stand my ground and continue.

"You've always been tenderhearted, Lane. But please allow me to have a mom moment. I've come to know Kevin over the past few months. He is indeed a nice man. But he also has some serious baggage. Just be careful."

"It is just dinner with friends. That's all," she emphatically stated.

This time when Kevin knocked, Lane answered the door. After a brief conversation that included Peter, the two of them said goodbye and walked towards the pedestrian bridge leading to downtown and Amore.

Fortunately, Peter and I had plans as well. Otherwise, I would undoubtedly have spent the evening fretting over my daughter's interest in an FBI Agent. We donned our coats and crossed the street to the Webers' for dinner and an evening of cards. Jean greeted us, apologizing that Randall would be a few minutes late. Apparently, he had been at the office most of the day trying to meet a deadline.

Peter and I jumped in to help with final preparations for the evening's meal. Keeping to our on-going pact of low stress meals (except of course for the upcoming Beef Bourguignon), Jean was in the process of laying out a spread for street tacos. Peter took over the chopping of vegetables as I tended the stir fry of diced chicken and Jean pulled condiments out of the refrigerator. Millie

The Neighborhood

took care of any scraps that ended up on the floor. The margaritas we sipped as we executed our tasks probably helped boost the relaxed and jovial nature of the evening. Randall showed up just as we were about to pour a second round. I watched the stress dissolve from his face as he joined the camaraderie of the group.

After dinner, the four of us sat down for an evening of gin rummy. Over the years we had cycled through a variety of card games, but this seemed to be our fallback, and favorite. At some point, we had started keeping tabs on the winners. We played women against men. Each February we tallied the past year's results. The losing team owed the winners an evening out. Although the card game itself never felt overly competitive, the stakes had become quite high. In the beginning, the "prize" had been a nice dinner out but over the years, the winners had been treated to concerts, spa days and fly-fishing outings. With only a few weeks left until we named the winners, the guys were slightly ahead.

Our unspoken rule during our card games was that there was to be no work-related talk unless it involved travel plans. So, the conversation floated over a variety of topics, mostly light hearted, laced with laughter. At some point, the topic of Dmitry's impending visit emerged. I had not realized until tonight how often Randall's and Dmitry's paths had crossed over the years. Between he and Peter, they regaled us with many stories of Dmitry's exploits.

It wasn't until the last round of cards that Randall said, "So Peter, I understand you are now the keeper of 'the general's' notebook." My FBI Asset ears perked up.

"Apparently so," Peter said with a smile as he played his hand. "You two had better be careful. But don't worry, I plan to rule more as a benevolent dictator than a general."

"Anything in particular that Jean and I should be aware of 'Sir'?" Randall quipped with a salute.

"Actually, I haven't looked through the book. Evelyn hid it from me as soon as it was in her hands. Perhaps she is going to hold a coup and take over before I can even establish my rule."

All eyes were on me expecting a witty response to this banter.

Torn between continuing the conversation in hopes of gleaning information or ending it before additional suspicion was cast upon these dear friends, I opted for a compromise.

"The monarchy of Queen Evelyn will restore harmony and goodwill throughout the neighborhood," was about the wittiest thing I could think of to say at this point. "Actually, I haven't read the book either. Bill always meant well, but his neighborhood critiques could be off-putting. I decided it was best not to know what was said, especially about Peter and me. The book currently is gathering dust in a closet and there it shall remain."

We had just finished the last round of cards with Jean and me proving triumphant this evening, when there was a knock at the door. To everyone's delight (except perhaps mine) were Lane and Kevin. Jean ushered the two of them in and offered to make a new pitcher of margaritas. To my surprise they gratefully accepted. I followed Jean into the kitchen, knowing her curiosity was piqued. I had purposely not mentioned Lane's evening plans, hoping to avoid the speculation about a budding romance.

"You are holding out, my friend," Jean led with.

"I'm not sure what you mean," I evasively said. "Lane just wanted to introduce Kevin to a few of her friends who are still in town. Help him develop a social base. That's all there is to it."

As the blender whirred, Jean looked me straight in the eyes and stated, "Evelyn, you are either in denial or just plain blind. Lane might not even be aware, but she is falling for him. You can see it in her eyes when she looks at him. I thought you liked Kevin."

"I do like Kevin," I answered honestly. "I just think he is carrying a lot of baggage from his divorce and I don't want to see Lane caught up in it."

The Neighborhood

"It's not going to be your decision," Jean bluntly said.

As the six of us sat and sipped our drinks, Lane and Kevin shared the latest adage from Miss Essie. They had run into her at the restaurant where she was enjoying a triple dip ice cream sundae. Kevin had commented that was a lot of ice cream.

Offering her best Miss Essie impersonation, Lane pushed her imaginary glasses up her nose and said, "Young man, there is always room for ice cream. It melts and fills in the crevices!"

Amidst our laughter, Peter offered a toast to such wise advice. As we cheerfully raised our glasses, I found myself closely watching Kevin and Lane. Although fleeting, I caught the milli-second when their eyes met and there was recognition of a shared memory, the type of experience that begins to bond two people. If I was to watch objectively, I had to agree with Jean's analysis. I could read my daughter very well and whether she realized it or not she was definitely smitten with Kevin. What I didn't know was at what level those feelings were being genuinely reciprocated.

The next morning, I was greeted with two equally upsetting pieces of news. The first came in the form of a text on my burner phone.

The surveillance camera picked up someone entering your house last night, but we couldn't get a clear visual of who. Whoever it was knew to stay in the shadows. Have you noticed anything moved in the house?

A chill ran down my spine, as the reality set in that someone had broken into my home. Of course, I knew it was a possibility someone might come looking for the notebook, at least in concept. But to know it had actually happened was something totally different. For the first time since my double life began, I found myself afraid.

What incriminating evidence was in 'the general's' notebook? Once again, I found myself taking deep, calming breaths as I slowly walked through the house looking for any sign someone had been in the house. In the back of my mind was the nagging awareness that Randall had arrived late for dinner last night. That, coupled with his query about 'the general's' notebook, was unsettling. I was scanning the desks in our office when the doorbell rang.

Kamya was at the door, her eyes red and swollen. "We received news that our nephew passed away last evening. Manasi and I will be traveling to India. If you would watch the house, we would appreciate it." Her voice broke as she struggled to share the heart-breaking news.

As I enveloped her with my arms, she once again broke into tears. I ushered her into the kitchen where I put the kettle on for a cup of tea. In times of grief, I know how important it is for people to tell their story. I sipped my tea as Kamya began to talk.

Over the next thirty minutes, she laid out the journey the family had been on over the past decade. Their nephew's father had been scheduled to make the kidney donation to his son. Tragically, Manasi's brother was killed in a house fire leaving his organs unharvestable. "Manasi was serving as interim head of Global Health Biotech; you know he had served as director there before we moved to Deep Fork. Anyway, he was trying to help them through a rough patch. The Russian mafia was leveraging their muscle trying to divert funds. The stress of that, coupled with his brother's sudden death, nearly broke Manasi." I sat quietly as she paused and looked off into the distance for several minutes. "It was during that time we found out Manasi was a good match for our nephew. He resigned his interim position and we went to India where he donated a kidney. Manasi was quite fond of his nephew before this. However, after the kidney transplant the two became exceptionally close. Abhay was only thirty-six. He leaves behind a wife and young son."

I offered one last hug as she left and agreed to look after their house while they were gone. Once again, I reflected on a refrain that seemed to be playing through my mind often these days, *there are many ways to lose a child.*

The Neighborhood

I arranged to meet Kevin later in the day after Lane had left and Peter was absorbed in whatever book he was currently reading. The three of us attended church where I lifted up the Patel family, praying for the healing presence that comes from being surrounded by loved ones.

Chapter 24

As was my custom when weather permitted, I took a long Sunday afternoon walk. Unfortunately, now my walk served as a ruse to enter Kevin's house via the creek path. Apparently, the unseasonably warm day had inspired others to enjoy the beautiful weather as well. The path was quite busy, mainly with students from the university. A little nervous I might be observed as I headed towards my rendezvous, I once again became aware of how invisible I was among the young outdoor enthusiasts. Pretending to tie my shoe, I stopped at the end of the path leading to Kevin's house. A quick look confirmed no one seemed aware of my presence. I quickly turned and disappeared into the cedar trees bordering Kevin's property.

I quickly brought him up to date concerning the Patels' situation. Information he had collected from other sources as well as information gathered through the planted surveillance devices, confirmed Kamya's story. Kevin once again handed me the red marker and I was able to eliminate another couple from the Evidence Board. It had been less than a month since I first viewed this wall of evidence. At the time, Peter and I were the only ones sporting a red X. Now, the Patels could join the Jungs and the Barretts among those whose names had been cleared. The smiling faces of the two remaining couples hauntingly gazed back at me.

I also filled him in on the previous evening's conversation

The Neighborhood

concerning 'the general's' notebook. This prompted him to pull up the surveillance video. Sure enough, someone was letting themselves in through our side garage door. As Kevin had indicated, the individual was shrouded in darkness and obviously knew to hug the side of the house where detection would be less possible. All that could really be detected was a blurred image. What we did have was a time stamp. The perpetrator entered around 7:15 pm and stayed approximately 10 minutes.

"What time did you get to the Webers' last night?" Kevin questioned.

"We arrived around 7:00." I knew the next bit of information I was about to share could prove incriminating for Randall. "But, Randall was still at the office and didn't arrive till about 7:30."

Kevin quickly made a note on a post-it and added it to the evidence board. Although it could be coincidence, I was painfully aware of how convenient it was for the Webers to know with certainty we would not be at home. Was our evening together just a ploy to give Randall an opportunity to search for 'the general's' notebook? The knot in my stomach that had become my constant companion, tightened.

"Let's talk about Dmitry's visit," Kevin diplomatically changed the focus.

"He is due to arrive late Tuesday afternoon. Since he has never been here before, he asked Peter for an extensive tour of Deep Fork University. That should take most of the day on Wednesday. The Webers will join us that evening for dinner. He's scheduled to leave Thursday morning." That was really all the information I had regarding the visit of an apparent recruiter of Russian agents.

"The timing of Dmitry Sergey's visit is just too coincidental. Have you been able to ascertain any more information of what brings him to the States?"

"No, just that it is related to business," I stated.

"I'm sure whatever reason he gave is just a cover. It's going to be imperative that we track as much of his visit as possible. You will have eyes on him for at least part of the visit. I'll need you to keep thorough notes and create a timeline detailing where he is, who he is with and any comments he makes regarding his plans while in town. I've requested an additional agent who will tail Sergey as well. I plan to strategically place myself on campus hoping to have some interaction during his visit. With any luck we will find a discrepancy or movement that will lead us to the purpose for his visit."

I listened intently to my assignment making mental notes of what I needed to do whilst also preparing a Julia Child's recipe. I had a feeling I would need a little extra time on my yoga mat to achieve the focus I would need over the next few days.

"You haven't mentioned the bugs we planted for a while. Have you heard anything else of interest?"

"I've terminated the devices that were planted in the homes of the three couples who have been taken off our list. The Webers seem excited about Dmitry's visit. There have been several references to Dmitry over the past few days, especially after your conversation over cards."

"I'm still perplexed by the lack of conversation between the Andersons," he continued. "Cynthia left this morning for St. Louis. The little bit of conversation we have detected makes it appear this was an unplanned trip. I had intended to have an agent track her on her next St. Louis trip, but it happened so quickly I was unable to get it scheduled."

"It's not uncommon for Cynthia to take a quick trip to St. Louis," I reflected. "Is there a possibility a bug could be planted on Dmitry? It seems like that would be an easy way to see who he is meeting with."

"I've considered it. Naturally, the concern is that he would find it, tipping off the sleeper agents to the investigation. They would likely pull out and we could lose vital intel on other cells operating in the USA."

"I guess I had not thought of the broader implications," I murmured as I let this information sink in. "I noticed some additional notes on both the Webers' and Andersons' profiles. Is this information you gleaned from 'the general's' notebook?"

"Yes, a couple of interesting items, which I am pursuing. First off, there are several references to the Webers' dog, Millie. As irritated as Bill Walker might have been with many of his neighbors, he had a great affection for the dog. There are several notations about taking treats over for the dog. One of his last entries refers to a time he walked up on the Webers in the midst of an argument. Jean was visibly upset about something and used the term bardak. All we have is Mr. Walker's spelling of the word so it will take a bit of time to come up with colloquiums that match it. However, it does sound Russian. As innocuous as it may seem, slip ups like that often prove valuable."

"With the Andersons, there seems to be an issue with water draining from their yard into the Walkers'. The first reference to this was last spring. Apparently, nothing was done to address the issue, so Mr. Walker made a note to begin the conversation in the new year in anticipation of spring rains. His notebook showed he left a phone message on the 7th of January. That was one of the last notations he made..."

"before he was murdered," I finished the sentence for Kevin. I suddenly felt very tired and found myself just wanting to retreat to the comfort of my home and cuddle on the couch with my husband.

"Also," Kevin sheepishly said, "I was going over last night's audio surveillance from the Webers' house. It picked up the conversation you and Jean had concerning my relationship with Lane."

"And…." I decided he needed to take the lead on this conversation.

"I can't speak for Lane's feelings. I can only address my own. I don't deny I find your daughter very attractive and am developing fond feelings for her. But I assure you, this is as far as I will let things go until this investigation is completed." I know his words were meant to reassure me but in fact they only raised a myriad of other questions in my mind.

"I really don't know what to do with this information," was the most honest response I could give.

"You don't have to do anything with it. Just trust me." Strangely, these words did reassure me, at least to a point. If I had learned anything about Kevin over the past month, it was that he was a man of his word.

As I made my way home along the creek path, my head was spinning with all of the information I had processed over the past hour and a half. Dmitry was coming which meant something was ramping up, tidbits of information I had gathered seemed to be incriminating two of my closest friends and, oh, by the way, an undercover FBI agent might be falling in love with my daughter. My head really hurt!

Absorbed in my thoughts, I nearly ran full on into Victor Anderson. He looked equally surprised to see me.

"Victor! it's a beautiful day for a walk."

"Yes. It is beautiful," he barely broke stride as he continued his walk.

I turned to watch him and remembered Kevin once telling me, "The best spies are nice guys." In that case, Victor was in the clear.

Chapter 25

Dmitry was due to arrive just before dinner. I'd spent the day doing as much advance preparation as possible for tomorrow evening's meal and had just turned my attention to cleaning the mess I'd incurred, when Peter walked in the door.

"It smells wonderful in here," he said appreciatively as he gave me a big hug. "Have you been channeling Julia?"

"I thought I better get the bulk of the cooking done today since I have class tomorrow. Julia's Beef Bourguignon is one of the few recipes worthy of spending the day preparing. I think I have used every pot in the kitchen," I said ruefully as I looked at the pile of dirty dishes in the sink.

"You go lie down for a bit. I'll take care of the dishes. It can be my contribution to what will be a fabulous meal," he offered. I really am blessed to have a considerate husband. He always has my back, even when it comes to dishes. I couldn't help but wonder how he would take the news of my double life. Or perhaps, he would never know. Once, Kevin had commented we were playing a long game. What did that mean? Were we talking month or years? Would I keep this secret my entire life only for it to come to light when my memoir was published? I took Peter's advice and laid on my bed and pulled a blanket over my head. At least for a few minutes, I wanted to hide from the world.

Dmitry arrived just before 5:00 pm boasting a big smile and lots of hugs. I truly was finding it quite difficult to reconcile the Dmitry I had come to know over the years with the implications of his international espionage role. Although I know Peter and Dmitry stay in contact via e-mail, I am always surprised how easily they fall back into their friendship. The camaraderie the two of them share is palpable, although the conversation might have been boosted with the vodka Dmitry gifted us with.

Around 7:00 pm we donned our coats, scarves and gloves and began the walk towards Amore. It was a beautiful Oklahoma evening. Although cold, it was not bone chilling. There was not a cloud in the sky, giving us a spectacular view of the stars. Having spent most of his time in large cities, Dmitry expressed true appreciation for nature's light show. "Arranged it just for you!" Peter offered. "Next time you visit, I'll schedule a thunderstorm. Watching the night sky illuminated with lightening is truly spectacular."

"But no tornadoes, my friend," Dmitry joked. "I don't need to see cows flying through the air." Hollywood has certainly created a unique visual of Oklahoma. Although I often find myself feeling defensive at this characterization of my adoptive state, Peter simply said, "Deal." Steering my mind back on course, I focused on keeping a mental note of everything being said. Kevin had tasked me with reporting back details of our conversations, and if I am anything, I am a rule follower. However, I found myself wondering how much witty banter I should include. I couldn't see how the bad puns and walks down memory lane the two enjoyed could aid in our investigation.

Entering the restaurant, the owner, Paolo, cordially greeted us and led the three of us to an intimate table towards the back of the dining room. Linen table cloths, candlelight and fresh flowers on each table created a homey atmosphere. The restaurant was unusually busy for a Tuesday evening. As we made our way to our table, we waved at several friends from the university and church.

"I think the two of you have many friends," Dmitry observed.

"The benefit of living in a small town for many years," Peter's comment was laced with a deep sense of contentment. "Deep Fork was the right choice for Ev, Lane and me." I was grateful to hear Peter confirm what I had always felt. We both knew there were many career paths we could have followed, many places we could have lived. But to reach this point in our lives and feel we had chosen wisely was quite satisfying.

I can be a creature of habit when it comes to ordering at a restaurant. For the past few years, Peter and I had taken to sharing an entrée or only eating half of what was put in front of us and enjoying the leftovers the following evening. However, we had both agreed this evening we would take full advantage of the menu and ensure our guest enjoyed all that Amore had to offer.

Relishing the fact that his restaurant was hosting an international businessman, Paolo chose to wait on us himself. He was delighted when we ordered a bottle of wine and indicated we would start with an antipasto plate as we perused our entrée options. "And a salad?" he guardedly queried.

"After our entrée, to cleanse our palate," Peter winked.

"You order like a true Italian this evening," Paolo said approvingly.

Once our entrée decisions had been made and the order placed, we settled into an evening of relaxed conversation, wine and food. At least that is what my two male companions were experiencing. I felt bathed in anxiety about my role in uncovering the true goal of Dmitry's visit.

We had just finished our antipasto plate when a familiar voice said, "This looks like a fun table." I looked up to see a smiling Cynthia with Victor hovering behind her.

"Cynthia! I thought you were in St. Louis," I said a little too quickly. Was I supposed to know that? It could be my imagination but I thought she gave me a curious look.

"I just returned. It was a quick trip to check on my aunt," she responded. Turning her gaze to Dmitry she graciously extended her hand and said, "Hello, I am Cynthia Anderson and this is my husband Victor."

"Dmitry Sergey, pleased to meet you," Dmitry said as he stood and shook her hand. Turning to Victor he extended his hand, "and you as well, sir."

"Dmitry is a friend from my foreign exchange days in Germany," Peter offered.

"How wonderful to share time with friends," Cynthia continued focusing her attention on Dmitry.

"Yes, Peter and Evelyn are the best!" He answered raising his glass as if to toast us. "And this fine Italian food is a delightful surprise!"

"From your accent I would guess you are not from around here," she congenially continued.

"No, my home country is Russia but now I consider myself a citizen of the world," Dmitry shared, oozing charm.

"We've never visited Russia. It seems like such an interesting country. I've always been intrigued with the architecture of Saint Petersburg," Cynthia politely offered.

As had become my custom since becoming an asset to the FBI, I used this interaction to observe the key players, looking for any statement or nuance that might tip the scales in one direction or another in identifying the Russian agents. There was absolutely nothing incriminating or suggestive in the conversation that was taking place in front of me. In fact, it was a totally appropriate conversation that might take place between casual acquaintances. Yet, the whole thing felt staged. A little too perfect. Although Victor was never one for small talk, he seemed more uncomfortable than usual when placed in social occasions. In fact,

The Neighborhood

as soon as there was a lull in the conversation, he took Cynthia's elbow said a quick goodbye and steered her out of the restaurant. But what struck me the most about the whole interchange was that it was the first time I could ever remember seeing the two of them touch. Most married couples I knew might not be overtly affectionate, but there is an intimacy that comes from sharing lives together. The hand on the small of a back as you move through a crowd, touching of an arm as you share a story or perhaps brushing lint off a shoulder. I suddenly realized I had never sensed any affection between the Andersons. In many ways they seemed to coexist. Whether this was related to them being spies or just an unfulfilling marriage, or both, was to be determined. Once again, I found myself grateful for the relationship Peter and I shared.

Our meal stretched out over a two-and-a-half-hour period filled with excellent cuisine, laughter, stories and more wine than Peter and I consume in a month.

Walking home, I fell behind Peter and Dmitry as we crossed the pedestrian bridge. I've always been a bit obsessed with observing people's walks. Something so distinct for each person, and yet, we never actually witness our own walk. This was the thought rolling through my wine infused brain as I watched the two of them. Friends for nearly forty years, they both had what I would term 'confident' walks. Dmitry's walk could almost be described as a swagger. No doubt, he was used to commandeering any room he entered and expected to be the center of attention. Peter, on the other hand, exuded a confidence of someone who, as the French would say, 'was comfortable in his own skin'. Although a few inches shorter than Dmitry, he walked tall, swinging his arms broadly.

We were quickly approaching our house when I heard Dmitry ask, "Where did they find the body of your friend? What did you call him, 'the general'?" Peter waved in the general direction of the creek, "Just behind Randall's house. His wife Jean was out walking their dog, Millie, and found our neighbor's body."

"So very sad. I think someone his age should not be out walking alone." Even though my brain felt a little foggy, something felt off about his remarks. First, when did Peter tell Dmitry about 'the general'? I didn't recall it as part of the evening's conversation. Until this moment, it had not occurred to me that Dmitry was fully aware of all that had and might be about to happen. Why was he here? No sooner had the thought run through my mind, than Peter asked what I had been thinking. How is that for marriage telepathy?

Since I couldn't share my real thoughts I simply said, "Dmitry, you haven't told us what brings you to our corner of the world."

"For me, it is always business!!! I have colleagues who are interested in oil exploration in Russia. I am working my 'Dmitry Magic' with some Texas based oil companies. You are as they say 'a stone's throw' from Dallas. Of course, I would want to see one of my oldest friends and his beautiful wife." Always the charmer!

Although exhausted, I performed my assigned espionage duties, writing a synopsis of the evening's conversation. I was sure to include the encounter with the Andersons, incorporating my observations and reflections on their relationship, and Dmitry's comments regarding 'the general'. Then quite gratefully, I fell into a deep slumber.

Chapter 26

After a late night, and too much wine, all three of us were moving sluggishly the next morning. I laid out a continental breakfast of sorts with muffins and scones made by our local bakery, fruit and coffee...lots of coffee. Peter had arranged his day to give Dmitry a VIP tour of all that Deep Fork University had to offer. I know Peter is proud of the international studies program he has built through the Hanser Center and was anxious to share it with his friend. He also confided in me that he wanted Dmitry to understand the scope of the research done through the university. "You never know when Dmitry's contacts might benefit a program here at DFU." Little did he know what ramifications might exist because of Dmitry's contacts!

Once Peter and Dmitry left, I tidied up the kitchen and gathered what I would need for my class. I was just pulling out of the driveway when I saw Kevin hailing me down. Rolling down my window, we greeted each other as neighbors would. Poking his head in the window he asked how last evening had gone.

"I've written everything out. Nothing really telling as far as I can see. Peter and Dmitry have already left for campus," I said.

"Yes, I watched them leave. I've scheduled an IT visit in Peter's office in thirty minutes. I'm hoping to catch the two of them. An agent is already in place on campus. Any idea what their itinerary might be for the day?" He inquired.

"They are starting at the Hanser Center. Peter is eager to for

Dmitry to see the full scope of the international travel programs. The other major item on their schedule is touring the Whiteley Research Center."

"Good to know. Perhaps there will be an IT issue there this afternoon," he offered with a grin. With that, he waved good bye.

Today was one of the rare times I did not give a hundred percent to my students. I found myself preoccupied with thoughts of espionage, betrayal and, of course, the evening's meal. Fortunately, the class was so engaged with the discussion over the Tulsa Race Riots of the 1920's that my input was minimally needed. Good literature + compelling theme = interesting discussion. A tried and true formula!

Arriving home about 1:00 pm, I decided a thirty-minute power nap would be to my benefit. As I lay on the sofa with my eyes closed, my mind flitted from one thought to the next. Had 'the general' seen something that prompted his murder? Was Lane falling for Kevin? Why was Jean mad at Randall? Was she cursing in Russian? Had I checked on how much amaretto we had for this evening's dessert? Should I make decaffeinated coffee or regular tonight? Where did Cynthia get the blouse she was wearing last evening? How often did she go to visit her aunt in St. Louis? Realizing I was not going to get the respite I craved, I got up and began setting the table for this evening's dinner.

Although I am not one to fuss over decorating my house, I do love a pretty table. I find the process of laying out linens and tableware very calming and the reflection of candlelight off of glassware almost magical. For tonight's meal, I chose an ivory fringed throw laying it diagonally over the freshly polished Amish style dining table. The warm woods against the textured tablecloth gave a palette I could build from. Keeping in the vein of the heavy meal I was preparing, I pulled out a set of earth-toned pottery plates I had found at a garage sale a few years ago. I didn't use them often since they had to be hand washed but felt this occasion called for them. In the end, I felt great satisfaction with the vibe the table was giving off. Casual yet classy. The addition of candlelight would put the final touches on the ambiance I was hoping to achieve.

By the time I pronounced the table finished, it was half past three. Jean had offered to bring the appetizer, which meant I only had to put the beef bourguignon in the oven to slow cook over the course of the afternoon. I had debated whether I should make a salad but decided to go with Julia's suggestion of buttered peas. In addition, we would have buttered noodles and fresh bread from our local bakery. All in all, it would be a quite rich meal, not heart healthy at all. But I was going for flavor and in the words of Julia Child, "You can never have too much butter."

I checked the time and confirmed I had a few minutes for some deep breathing exercises hoping to calm my anxiety about the upcoming evening. Which, actually, I found myself resenting. A month ago, a dinner with three of our closest friends would have been sheer delight. Now it only held the promise of angst and deceit. For the umpteenth time, I checked the time. Peter and Dmitry should be home in the next forty-five minutes. The Webers' would arrive around 6:30 pm. I decided to throw some cold water on my face as one more attempt to brace myself for the evening when the doorbell rang. I don't know why I was surprised to see Cynthia at my door; after all she had been here many times before, but today I felt wary. But of course, ever mindful of my neighborly manners, I invited her in for a cup of tea, which she readily accepted.

"What a beautiful table," she admiringly noted as we passed through the dining room into the kitchen. "And it smells absolutely splendid."

"Thank you. I'm fixing Beef Bourguignon for dinner. Dmitry has eaten in some of the best restaurants in the world, so I'm feeling a bit of pressure to put my best foot forward," I admitted.

"If the smell is any indication, you have no need to worry," she said kindly. "I didn't realize you're having a dinner party so I'll pass on the tea, but I did want to ask if you have had any word on the Patels?"

"Not since our visit Sunday. It's so sad about their nephew. I suspect they will be gone for several weeks. Kamya asked me to water her plants and bring in the mail."

"That's so kind of you. You are a good friend Evelyn," Cynthia said. "Actually, I stopped by hoping you might have an address in India where I could send a card." Again, I was reminded of the kindness and sensitivity of my neighbor.

"Actually, I do, it is in the office. Let me go get it for you."

"Do you mind if I read over your bourguignon recipe while you get the address? It smells so delicious. Victor would love it."

As I rifled through the papers on my desk to find the Patels' India address, I found myself pleased that Cynthia was wanting to prepare something special for Victor. Perhaps I had misread their marriage.

The Webers arrived promptly at 6:30 pm with appetizers and two bottles of wine. Added to the two bottles I had already purchased, I felt we were well, if not overstocked, for the evening.

The dinner conversation floated from one subject to the next with a lot of laughter laced throughout. Dmitry had been quite impressed with the research happening at DFU and was complimentary to Randall about the quality of faculty he had been able to recruit.

"This DARPA project you have should elevate your university to a very high level, I think," Dmitry praised. "Well done," he continued as he raised his glass in a toast.

"So, you were able to give Dmitry a full tour of the facility?" I queried as I took a sip of wine.

The Neighborhood

"Indeed! We spent the better part of the afternoon talking with Gary, Jin and Victor. I know my IQ about the DARPA grant was raised today," Peter cheerily shared. I'll admit my heart sunk a bit as my husband naively continued, "We really have recruited some top-notch scientists."

"Speaking of top notch, you should be proud of your international studies program, my friend," Dmitry complimented. Peter grinned from ear to ear as Dmitry continued to praise the program and the ramifications it would have on the students' future world view. I know our Russian friend knows how to lay on flattery, but his affection and admiration of my husband resonated as genuine.

"I also met Lane's beau today," Dmitry declared. I froze mid-drink whilst Jean giggled and Randall and Peter exchanged a smile. "Excuse me," I said.

"Oh, come on, Evelyn, are you the only one who doesn't see the growing attraction between Kevin and Lane?" Jean asked. Looking around the table, I realized perhaps I was. Or perhaps I just did not want to admit it to myself.

"Whether there is something there or not, it is still in the early stages. Time will tell if it will develop into something," I shared, trying to shut down any further discussion.

"But you like this Kevin, yes?" Dmitry asked. "He seems like a very nice young man. Tall, good looking with a boyish charm and smart as well. He was able to fix the internet problems as you Americans would say 'lickety-split'."

It wasn't until we were enjoying our dessert that Dmitry turned his attention toward Jean. "I do not wish to cloud our lovely evening with sadness, but I understand you were the one who found your neighbor's body a few weeks ago. I am so very sorry. It must have been quite upsetting for you." I wondered if anyone else felt this was an awkward twist in what had been a very relaxed and upbeat evening.

"Yes, I was walking our Golden Retriever when we found the

body. So very tragic. Millie has been depressed ever since."

"How did he come by this name 'the general'?" asked Dmitry.

Peter answered this query. "Bill was retired military, I'm not sure what his final rank was. However, he earned the title general because of his inspection of the neighborhood. He patrolled daily, keeping track of lawn care, renovations, trash cans. You name it, he saw it. It wasn't until after he died that we found he actually kept a notebook about his inspections."

"That's right. The torch has been passed to Peter," Randall said with a wink.

"You are now the keeper of the notebook?" Dmitry asked.

"Bill's widow gave it to Ev. Since we are some of the longest residents of the neighborhood, she thought we would want to continue his work. Our own version of neighborhood watch," grinned Peter.

"So exactly what is in the notebook?" asked Jean.

"Ev will have to answer that. I haven't even seen the infamous notebook," said Peter.

All eyes turned to me. I realized I needed to choose my words carefully. If one or more of the people wanted to get their hands on the notebook, I needed to make sure they understood it was not easily accessible.

"Actually, I have not opened it. Perhaps I am a little nervous about what 'the general' might have said about Peter and me." I hoped my smile looked genuine as I spoke. "At any rate, I put it in a box and moved it to the attic. Perhaps someday it will see the light of day, but that day is not today." Not a total lie. I had not read the notebook. However, it currently resided in the hands of the FBI and not in my attic.

The Neighborhood

Chapter 27

Considering all that was transpiring, I slept surprisingly well. Wine, a full belly and the exhaustion that comes with leading a double life led me to sleep like a log. Dmitry was scheduled to leave early in order to catch his Tulsa flight so I half-heartedly roused myself out of bed for our farewells. I would have preferred pulling the covers over my head and hiding from the world into which I had recently been transported. When I entered the kitchen Dmitry and Peter were sipping their coffee.

"Dmitry's checking his schedule to see if he and Tonya can meet us in Greece this summer," Peter chirped happily as he poured a cup of coffee for me.

"Wonderful!" I replied as I took a sip of coffee hoping my reaction came across as genuine. With a bit of luck, all this spy business would be well behind me by the time we crossed the Atlantic Ocean this summer.

Peter and I stood in the driveway waving goodbye as Dmitry's rental car headed out of the neighborhood. "I hope Dmitry got what he came for," Peter said reflectively.

I could barely contain my surprise at Peter's statement. Did he know more about Dmitry's double life than he let on? "What do you mean?"

"Don't get me wrong, I really like the guy and I think he truly wanted to visit us. But in my experience, Dmitry rarely does something that doesn't have an agenda, usually to his advantage. His interest in the Whiteley Research Center and their DARPA contract felt over the top, even for Dmitry. Time will tell." With that, he headed into the house.

Processing what Peter had just said, I was aware of the now familiar sound of running feet coming up from behind. No need to turn around, I thought, it's Kevin.

"We need to talk," Kevin said barely out of breath.

"A storm is coming in this afternoon so that negates me coming to your house via the creek path. Let's plan to meet at Walmart. What time?" I asked.

"3:00." And he was off.

Slipping into Kevin's car at our designated spot, I donned the ball cap that had become my disguise. We wove our way out of town to the wild life refuge where we could visit in private. The gathering storm clouds seemed to be a metaphor for the current situation.

"Give me a rundown of the evening," Kevin ordered.

I quickly outlined the previous night's conversation highlighting in Peter's words "Dmitry's over the top interest in the Whiteley Research Center."

"Yes, I witnessed part of the tour and discussion Dmitry had with various faculty. He was quite profuse with his compliments. Definitely a gregarious guy. Seems to demand attention wherever he goes," Kevin noted.

"He also mentioned the 'the generals' death. This was the second time he brought it up since he has been here. Although it was a tragedy, I found it curious he circled around to it," I reflected.

The Neighborhood

"Keep in mind that as far as the public is concerned, Mr. Walker's death was an accident. Only a handful of people know it was murder. This might have been Dmitry's way of putting out feelers to see if there is any suspicion in the community concerning the circumstances around his death." I waited while he made a few notes.

As he made notations, I contemplated who the short list of people in the know would be. Obviously, the police and coroner, Lauren who at least was suspicious, the two of us and of course the murderer. Once Kevin indicated he was ready, I continued. "First, Dmitry asked Peter and me about the accident and then he brought it up again with Jean last night. Peter mentioned the notebook, and that seemed to pique his interest. It also gave Jean an opportunity to question me about the notebook's content. Do you think they had planned this interchange to gather information?" I was suddenly aware of how contrived the conversation may have been. Again, I could feel my stomach tighten as I contemplated the knowledge that one of my dearest friends might be the guilty party.

"Interesting thought, double team approach," Kevin reflected. "What did you say?"

"I was able to say I had not read anything in the notebook," which was the truth, "and had placed it in a box which now resides in my attic. I'm hoping that detours anyone from looking for it."

"Well played. Depending on their concern over what the notebook may contain, they may or may not continue searching for it. But, if we detect someone going into the attic, we will know it is a limited number of folks who know that is where the notebook is allegedly kept."

Kevin really did not need to spell out who another break-in would implicate. There were only five people at the dinner table that evening, two of which occupied a space on the evidence board.

"Anything else of note from the evening's conversation?" Kevin queried.

"No, those are the highlights. I've also written a narrative of everything I can recall from Dmitry's visit. Nothing shouts out to me." I had chosen not to include the portion of the evening where we discussed his and Lane's budding relationship.

I had become fairly good at reading Kevin and sensed he'd been patiently letting me debrief concerning Dmitry's meeting. "So, what do you have to add?" I asked anticipating he had something important to share.

"Early this morning, around 2:00 am, our surveillance camera caught Dmitry exiting through your kitchen doors onto the veranda. He returned an hour and a half later. Our range was not able to pick up which direction he went, but obviously he was meeting someone. The question now is who?"

It took a few minutes for me to process this information. My home was becoming a hotbed of espionage. Peter's words from this morning rang like a bell in my mind, "I hope Dmitry got what he came for."

"Were you able to pick up anything from the bugs in the Andersons' and Webers' homes?" I cautiously asked, afraid to hear the answer.

"No, both houses were quiet throughout the night. Wherever the meeting took place was not inside one of their homes, at least not a part available to the public. I'm convinced there is a secret space in one of our suspect's homes."

"So, what is next?" I queried. "It feels to me as if things are coming to a head."

"I agree. I've been going through the intel we have gathered so far to construct a timeline which includes major events. I'm creating a theoretical scenario."

"Go on," I urged.

The Neighborhood

"The Russian cell has been planted for a long time. Ultimately, their purpose is the Whiteley Research Center. Although there was no guarantee the center would receive a DARPA grant, wheels have been in motion over the last decade to recruit the necessary scientists for that level of research work. Two key figures in making that happen are Randall Weber and Victor Anderson."

"What is perplexing," he continued, "are the two incidents that seemed to have escalated the cell's activity. Therein lies the key to identifying the agents. With the establishment of the DARPA center, their real work was only beginning."

"So, why tip their hand now?" I contemplated.

"I believe it all comes back to Bill Walker's notebook," Kevin thoughtfully responded.

The rain had just started as I pulled into my garage. The temperature would hover in the low 40's, meaning it would just be a cold rain, no ice or snow. Thankfully, there were enough leftovers from the previous evening for tonight's dinner. That, plus a crackling fire and downtime with my husband were just what the doctor ordered to soothe my frayed nerves.

Although I had cleaned up the majority of items from last night's party, I still had a few things to put away. In the process of picking up the table linens, I dropped a napkin. It was as I leaned over to pick it up, I saw it.

A month ago, I would have been perplexed by the small cylinder-shaped object attached to the underside of my table. Perhaps curious, but not concerned. Now, the bile in my stomach churned as I sank slowly to the floor. With my forehead pressed against the cold, hard edge of the table, I realized, once again my privacy had been invaded and this time by someone I called friend.

Chapter 28

With shaking hands, I typed a text into the burner phone notifying Kevin of the latest development. I was still waiting for a response when Peter walked in. Two late nights plus a day of catch up at work had taken their toll. He looked exhausted. I noticed he had not brought any work home, an abnormality for Peter, telling me just how tired he really was. We sat at the kitchen table eating leftovers in silence. Each of us lost in our own thoughts.

As I cleaned up from dinner, Peter stoked the fire and pulled up a murder mystery for us to stream. Knowing I was living my own version of a "whodunnit" movie, it really didn't matter what was playing in front of me. The chance of me focusing on the screen was nominal. Once again, I checked the burner phone. No message.

Peter fell asleep in his chair about forty-five minutes into the movie. As exhausted as I was, I knew sleep would not come easily for me this evening. I mindlessly continued to watch the movie, frequently checking for a response from Kevin.

His response finally came as the movie was ending. *When can we meet?*

I looked out the window at the cold, winter rain that was pouring down and decided I would not brave the weather this evening. I had decided to leave the listening device in place until I had conferred with Kevin. Therefore, meeting at my house was out of the question.

Tomorrow morning after Peter leaves for work.

Coffee shop at 8:30 am. Take a picture of the device making sure to capture any identifying marks.

I love the familiarity of the morning routine Peter and I have developed over the years. While some may consider it mundane, right now I craved the normality. Although we rarely spoke as we dressed and ate our morning meal, the entire ritual was infused with a sense of compatibility and security. The rain was still coming down as we readied ourselves to leave for the university. Deciding to carpool, I offered to drop Peter off, claiming I would be working from the coffee shop, at least for a few hours.

Focused on the screen of my computer, not really aware of what was in front of me, I heard the chipper voice of Kevin hail me from across the coffee shop. As I looked up, I smiled and waved him over. With the current speculation of his budding romance with my daughter, any passerby would see this as a 'schmoozing session' by a potential suitor.

Once seated, our conversation immediately turned towards this new development of the planted surveillance equipment. However, we both plastered smiles on our faces and did our best to maintain this farce of a casual tête-à-tête.

"Do you have any idea when this device might have been planted?" questioned Kevin.

"I found it under my dining room table as I was cleaning up after the dinner party. I'm fairly certain it was not there yesterday when

I was setting the table. I always wipe down and polish the table before setting it. I would have felt a device in the process of doing that."

"So that narrows our focus to Dmitry, Jean and Randall," Kevin speculated. "Correct?"

The needle was pointing more and more towards my dear friends. "Yes, I suppose so." I answered resignedly.

"There was no one else in your house yesterday afternoon and you did not leave for any length of time?" Kevin's question continued.

"I was there the entire time," I murmured. "Actually, Cynthia did stop by. She needed to get the Patels' address to send a sympathy card," I suddenly remembered.

"Was she left alone at any point?" he pressed.

"Just for a few minutes while I went into the office to get the address." Having done my own planting of bugs, I knew it took very little time to accomplish the task. "So, it could have been any one of them."

"Yes, but the question is why. Was it planted to get information you might have or that someone else would offer?"

"Such as Dmitry?" I queried.

"Unless he is the one who planted it," observed Kevin. "What information does someone feel you, or your guest, have that incriminates them. Once again, I believe it comes back to Bill Walker's notebook. I intend to spend the day garnering any information I can from its contents."

"What should I do about the bug? For now, it is still planted under my table." I'm sure he sensed my discomfort with this situation.

"Leave it. At this point, we don't want to tip anyone off that we have suspicions. Plus, there may be a way for us to turn it to our advantage."

"How so?" I really felt I already knew the answer to this.

"If our agents are this anxious to get their hands on the notebook, there will be another attempt to find it. We'll continue to use the surveillance equipment to monitor any movement," he explained.

"And if there is no attempt to find the notebook?" I asked as the caffeine in my coffee began to clear away the cobwebs that filled my mind. Was it lack of sleep, stress or confusion making me feel so unfocused today?

"It may be time for us to 'leak' information concerning the circumstances of Bill Walker's death," he stated slowly. "If our suspects feel there is about to be an investigation, it may force their hand." The way he carefully laid out this option, I knew it was a more dangerous scenario.

"Do you have a plan in mind?" I was afraid to know the answer to this.

"I'm working on it. Every scenario I have developed thus far has you revealing to our suspects the suspicion that Mr. Walker's death was murder," he shared. "I can't take the chance of having my identity revealed as of yet, but I do think it may be time to bring Peter into the fold. I will not launch any such plan until I feel we are fully able to protect the two of you."

Although Kevin's words were meant to reassure me, I could tell the smile on my face had frozen. I probably looked like one of those puppets you see in a marionette show, forced to smile with movement manipulated by someone else. I did not like this one little bit!

"You two are becoming an item." I looked up to see Cynthia Anderson standing over the two of us, smiling broadly. "I believe this is the second or third time I've seen you huddled over coffee."

Unfortunately, I was at a loss for a witty comeback. Kevin responded with a quick laugh, "I think we both know Evelyn hit pay dirt with Peter. He's a great guy."

"How did your Beef Bourguignon go over with your Russian guest?" Cynthia had turned her attention fully on me at this point. "I'm quite anxious to try your recipe."

"It was delicious. A lot of work but deserving of the accolades it always receives. Dmitry gave it five stars, a great review from someone as well traveled as him."

We exchanged a few more pleasantries about work and weather and then Cynthia was on her way. "It's hard to get a read on her," commented Kevin. "At times, I think she is overtly nosy but other times she comes across as sincerely interested in others."

"She has always been one to put the focus on others, let them talk about themselves. It's actually something I always admired about her. Now I'm just not sure."

We both sipped our coffee in silence for a few moments. Over the past few weeks, I had been forced to view friendships through a lens of suspicion and doubt. Normally, I considered myself a good judge of character. Now I found myself mistrusting even the most benign comments. I don't think I like the new me.

Kevin's voice cut through my contemplation. "When the time is right to read Peter in, I'll let you know." Obviously, the stress I was feeling showed on my face. "Evelyn, we will not move forward with a plan until you are comfortable with it. For now, continue with your normal routine." An ironic statement since nothing in my world was normal right now!

With that he picked up his coffee, stood and waved goodbye.

The Neighborhood

Chapter 29

Friday morning, I awoke to the second straight day of rain. The weather definitely matched the brooding mood I was in. I poured a cup of coffee and stared out the veranda doors to our rain-soaked lawn. In a few months, when crocuses and daffodils began to peek through, I'd be thankful for the moisture. However, today I yearned for warm temperatures, sunny skies and clarity.

Fences were rare in our neighborhood. Children and pets seemed to know appropriate boundaries and we all kept watch to make sure no child or animal was hurt. Over the years, we jokingly referred to it as our version of neighborhood watch. Because, until now, nothing nefarious had taken place in our little corner of the world. Reflecting over this as I sipped my coffee, my eyes moved towards the Anderson's house, the only adjoining property to boast a fence. As I recall, it was there when they moved to Deep Fork. In the far corner, I could see an area where rain had eroded under the fence creating a small river flowing into the Walkers' yard. Of course, that would have driven 'the general' crazy.

Normally I have class on Fridays, but today I'd given my students an assignment to visit the Tulsa Historical Society and Museum to learn more about the 1921 race riot. Often labeled as the worst race riot in American history, fifteen thousand blacks were left homeless and an estimated three thousand were killed, wounded or reported missing. This disturbing period of our state's history was a sobering experience for the students. Over the years, I found it better for them to experience the exhibit on their own rather than go collectively. Next week's discussions would focus on both their emotional and intellectual reactions to the exhibit.

Which meant I had a "found day." I had coined this term when Lane was small. It referred to a day when you unexpectedly find yourself without obligation. Snow days are a perfect example of a found day. As an adult it also happens when a meeting is cancelled or, in today's case, your work schedule changes. Since I had nothing pressing (well, except for the obvious task of saving democracy and foiling a potential plot to wage bio-terrorism), I decided to treat myself to a manicure and pedicure.

This little bit of luxury was a balm my soul badly needed. My morning drifted away as I soaked my feet in warm, soapy water, enjoyed hot towels wrapped around my freshly exfoliated legs, followed by a wonderful massage using lavender scented lotion. I even sprang for the extra hot stone massage option. By the time I had moved to the manicure chair I was already enjoying the benefits of this pampering. Two hours later, I left the salon my fingers and toes painted a cheery pink.

Knowing Peter would soon be pulled into my new world and Kevin would not implement any plans until they were fully vetted, I felt myself lulled into a false sense of security, and decided to take the weekend off from my 'spy gig'. Peter and I could enjoy a cozy evening at home and perhaps tomorrow drive to Tulsa to see a movie and go out for dinner. I was definitely feeling the need for a change of scenery. Just what the doctor ordered, I told myself as I used the remote to open the garage door and slowly pulled in.

Instinct is a funny thing. Although you can't put your finger on what is amiss, you sense some little thing is out of order. Whatever it was, the hairs on the back of my neck began to stand up as I stepped out of my car. As the garage door began to close behind me, I thought "I didn't do that." Then everything went dark.

The Neighborhood

Gradually I began to regain consciousness, acutely aware of a musty, dank smell. As my eyes rolled open, I blinked from the fluorescent light illuminating the concrete room. I was laid out on a cot in some type of bunker. My wet, muddy clothes were sticking to my body but that was not causing the chill coursing through my veins. Standing with their backs to me were Victor and Cynthia Anderson. Deciding it was best to play dead (not a good choice of words), I closed my eyes and listened.

"Why did you bring her here?" Asked a very agitated Victor.

The chill I felt was heightened by the sound of Cynthia's voice. Normally her tenor was sweet and kind. Her callous and harsh response to Victor's question confirmed what I already knew, I was in the presence of the enemy.

"We have to find the notebook. She's the only one who knows where it is." Cynthia sneered. "Our work is too important to have it ruined by nosy neighbors."

"You are out of control, Cynthia!" Victor hissed. "The old man was one thing, but this? Two murders in the same neighborhood in such a short time is going to make our work nearly impossible," he bluntly stated. "I have a meeting at the university I can't miss. Don't do anything until I return."

Fear overcame me as I realized my fate. Laying on the hard cot, I began to play through different scenarios in my mind. None of them ended well for me. As the two of them walked out of the bunker, I heard Cynthia's cold, calculating voice. "No one knows the old man was murdered. She can meet a similar tragic fate. But first, we must find the notebook." With that, the door clanged shut, and I heard the lock engage.

Once I was certain I was alone, I opened my eyes. I took several deep breaths trying to slow down the rapid, thumping of my heart. Although fear threatened to paralyze me, I turned, as I always had in times of trial, to prayer. I prayed for strength, clarity and to be rescued and then as, my father had taught me, began to assess my situation.

The room itself was approximately 10' x 10' and by the fact that I could see my breath, I knew it was not heated. The shudder that overtook my body was triggered by a combination of wet clothing, no heat and fear.

In many ways, the room was similar to the command center in Kevin's house. On one wall was an evidence board documenting research information related to both the DARPA and Whiteley Research Centers. Next to the board was a file cabinet with drawers categorized chronologically, beginning twelve years ago, when the Andersons arrived in Deep Fork. The bottom drawer was labeled 'Passports'.

Hanging on another wall were two black back packs. I assumed these were the infamous 'Go Bags' you see in spy movies. Next to the bags was a rack containing four guns which I had learned from Kevin were Glocks. Shelving next to the guns contained binoculars, cameras and surveillance equipment. An empty box labeled ammunition lay on its side. I made a note to check if the guns were loaded. Weapons without ammunition would not do me any good.

The third wall contained a desk with two computers and what looked like a satellite phone. Above this area was another board which held pictures of DFU faculty as well as neighbors. Again, like Kevin's evidence board, detailed notes accompanied each photo. How eerie it was to see a photo of myself smiling back at me. A framed photo of the current Russian president resided on the wall above the cot as well as newspaper clippings and posters, all in Russian.

As I pondered my fate, my father's voice came through loud and clear. "Evelyn, focus on the mission." I tried to sit up, but my head was bursting and I felt nauseated. Both my forehead and the back of my head ached intensely. Gently touching both areas, I could feel a stickiness which I assumed was congealed blood. Judging by the mud and tears on my clothing, I must have been dragged here. Suspecting I might have a concussion, I knew the worst thing I could do was to give in to the sleep my body was demanding. I forced myself to stand up and took a few minutes to gain my footing. First off, I checked the door to verify it was locked, which it was. Victor's statement about a meeting led me to believe I had a couple of hours before they would return, giving me time to formulate a plan.

Although I couldn't be positive, I assumed I was located in some type of underground shelter in the Andersons' yard. No doubt the cause of the drainage issue 'the general' had fretted over.

I started with the technology. Surely, I could make contact with the outside world, but the computers were both password protected and the satellite phone was not operable inside the concrete structure. Two strikes. However, I did notice some provisions and blankets under the cot. Good to know, I thought as my teeth chattered.

Although I was curious to explore the room, I knew my first priority was to find a way to protect myself and if possible, find an escape. The Go Bags! Surely, they would have something useful. Rifling through each bag I found a passport with new identities for the respective Andersons, cash, a burner phone (which required an activation code), flashlight, first aid kit and gun. I systematically checked each weapon confirming ammunition had been removed. I was more than a little frustrated to be surrounded by so much technology but unable to use it to my advantage.

I had just hung the second bag on the wall, when I heard the lock click open. I quickly returned to the cot and closed my eyes.

"No need to fake it. I know you're awake," Cynthia's voice cut through the room like ice.

Slowly I opened my eyes and looked at what I had once considered one of the sweetest ladies I knew. Boy, was I wrong.

"I don't understand." I said deciding to act as naïve as possible. "Where am I?"

"You know, Evelyn, I've always liked you. Unfortunately, your kindness has put you, for lack of a better word, in a 'grave' situation.' Quite simply, I need 'the general's' notebook and you are the only one who knows where it is."

"Why? It's just the ramblings of an old man." Although I knew it would not change my fate, I once again said, "I haven't even opened it."

"That may be the case. But, in the hands of certain people, information in that book could pose severe consequences for my cause."

"Your cause?" Although I was certain I knew the answer, the longer I could get her to talk, the more time I bought for myself.

"Look around, Evelyn. Does this look like a typical storm shelter?" She smirked.

Slowly, I looked around the room, taking in all of the paraphernalia contained in the bunker. "Who are you?"

"A down side of living a double life is that no one really knows the important work you do. For twelve years I've lived the persona of a supportive spouse, joining all the right clubs, making sure Victor makes the right connections to achieve our assigned goal."

"Assigned goal?" Again, I hoped playing dumb would buy me time.

"To restore Mother Russia to her former glory. Let me introduce myself. I am Vera Yerzova."

Chapter 30

In a weird way, I could relate to Cynthia's frustration at not being able to share what she was accomplishing through her secret life. To do so for twelve years would undoubtedly breed a desire and need to 'toot your own horn'. After all, I had only lived my double life for a few weeks. However, it probably wasn't a good idea to commiserate with her about our shared frustrations.

Strange that my reflective listening training was once again coming in handy. In this case, allowing a Russian spy to tell her story.

"As a drama student at the University of Moscow, I was a standout, showing incredible promise. My aptitude for accents is one of the reasons I was recruited for a top-secret sleeper cell program. A very prestigious honor. Playing the part of Cynthia Anderson has been the role of a lifetime for me. "

"You're a spy?" I made sure my voice sounded incredulous.

"But of course, comrade," she smiled broadly as she slipped into her native Russian accent.

"And Victor as well?"

"My first assignment was to recruit a brilliant physics student,

Kirill Denisov, to the program. You know him as Victor. It wasn't difficult. After all, how many geeky academics have a beautiful woman fawning over them. Men are easy. I believe the American term is pillow talk," she boasted.

"You must have been very young when you were recruited?" My voice quivered. The combination of fear and cold were intense.

"I was seventeen when my parents were killed in a car wreck. An uncle who was in the KGB recognized my talents and took me under his wing. He mentored me well."

"So, you and Victor married and became a spy couple?" Again, I wanted to keep her talking as long as possible.

Although she was smiling at me, I sensed the contempt in her voice. "Victor is not my husband. I am his handler."

As I allowed that bit of information to wash over me, I pushed for her to continue her story. "I don't understand. What are you doing in Deep Fork?"

"Seems crazy, yes. You Americans often don't see what is in front of you." With that she pointed at the board on the wall. "The Whiteley Research Center of course. Do you have any idea of the value of the work being done there? Victor has received credit for recruiting top scientists and landing the DARPA center. But it is me who really should be recognized. Without me, he is just another academic. It's been me who has researched and found scientists who have their own secrets, their own pasts. People who find a sense of security within the seclusion of this small town."

"My head is really hurting," which was true. "I don't understand what you are saying."

"Jin Jung, for instance. After I discovered he is a North Korean wanted for manslaughter, Victor was able to recruit him to DFU. The allure of a top-notch research facility with a low profile is very appealing for those with secrets of their own."

"Gary Barrett was another with a tragic past looking for a place to belong. It is my research, my work, my intelligence that is responsible for building the amazing team of scientists the center currently has. Victor simply does what I tell him."

Whether this was true or not, it was obvious Cynthia was a woman who had felt under-appreciated for a long time. She was also becoming more agitated as she shared her story. Although, I felt the longer she talked the better it was for me, I was racking my brain for a way to calm her down, at least a bit.

"I've always thought of you as a very smart woman," I threw out.

"Of course, I am smart. I am brilliant. This entire operation is possible because of me." As I tried to determine if I could use her inflated ego to my advantage, she veered in a different direction.

"All was going well until 'the general' got in the way."

"'The general'?" I asked, although I already knew what she was about to tell me.

"That meddlesome old man got what he deserved," she sneered.

"You killed him? Why?"

"This bunker was installed when we put in the storm shelter. Over the years, as the earth settled, a slope was created that unfortunately sends water draining into the Walkers' yard. He started grumbling about it last year and would just not let it go. About a month ago, he wandered into the garage looking for me so he could complain again. I was in here on the satellite phone. Unfortunately, to operate it we must keep the door to the bunker and storm shelter open. I was talking with my handler, when I turned around and found him standing in the room." The smile she gave me was anything but friendly, "As you may have guessed, no one who sees this room lives to talk about it."

I supposed it was time to address the elephant in the room. "You are going to kill me." It wasn't a question.

The Neighborhood

"But first I'll need the notebook." At least she was honest about it.

"What's in his notebook that is so incriminating?" I was stalling, sensing I was running out of time.

"Perhaps nothing, but I can't take that chance," she said matter of factly.

"Why should I tell you where the notebook is if you are going to kill me anyway?"

"Evelyn, there are many ways to die. Some are quick and relatively painless. Others take time and are excruciating. I'll leave you to decide your fate."

With that, she turned and left. By now, I was shivering uncontrollably. Cynthia's words played over and over, bringing to mind horrendous forms of torture. Again, praying for strength, I found a blanket under the cot, wrapped myself in it and forced myself to think through options. Again, I said a quick prayer and repeated the mantra, everything is figureoutable.

By my calculations, it was probably the middle of the afternoon. My guess was Victor would not return from the university until after 5:00 pm. Peter had often said, "You can set your watch by Victor Anderson. He leaves at 5:00 on the dot."

Peter, on the other hand, was a little less predictable. Occasionally on Fridays he would come home early; however, I knew he was behind on work due to Dmitry's visit. I assumed my car, purse and phone were all still in the garage. Hopefully, Peter would make it home and realize something was wrong. But I couldn't count on that scenario. As I used to tell Lane, "In life, you had better have a Plan A, B, C and be working on D. I needed to do whatever I could to save myself. Again, my dad's voice commanded, "Evelyn, think! How will you get out of this situation?"

Gingerly standing up, I once again explored the room for anything I could use to aid in my escape. What did I know about my prison? I'm underground, adjacent to a storm shelter. I assumed the Andersons' (or whatever their names were) shelter was like ours. I knew once I exited the bunker, I would have to climb a ladder out of the shelter.

If I could create some type of distraction when they entered the bunker, I might be able to escape. Glancing around the room, I noted all the moveable items. First off, I needed to move as many objects as I could to create tripping hazards. Leaning the cot against the wall by the door, I moved chairs, bags and rations to the center of the room. Planning to remove the overhead light, I was hoping at the very least they would trip their way through the room. That was Plan A.

Next, I needed to create some type of weapon I could use to hopefully knock one or both of them at least semi-unconscious. Knowing I was probably too weak to hit them with any force, I began an inventory of items in the room. As I looked around, a memory of my dad showing us how to fill a sock with coins to create a weapon surfaced. Unfortunately, I was wearing footies and there were no rolls of coins at my disposal, but there were small cans of food. I just needed something to hold them. Remembering a recent article about purses made from bras, I knew I had my vessel. I quickly unclasped my bra and pulled out each strap from under my wet sweater. Filling the cups with cans, wishing I was better endowed, I tied the two cups together creating a solid mass. I practiced swinging my improvised weapon to see how much and how quickly I could achieve the momentum I needed to hopefully render someone unconscious, or at the very least dazed. Luckily, the leverage didn't require much force to be effective.

I took one of the chairs and put it to the side of the door, propping the cot vertically against the chair. Fortunately, I had found a small flashlight in one of the go bags so when I disconnected the overhead light, I was not in total darkness. With Plan B in place, I prepared to wait.

Shining the flashlight around my jail, I tried to determine if there was anything else I could do. My last "line of defense" was to put several cans of a carbonated beverage near me. For the next few hours, I periodically shook these as I waited for my captors to return.

Chapter 31

The expression 'time stands still' certainly applies when you are sitting in a dark, freezing bunker with a probable concussion, waiting for someone to come and torture you. Knowing the worst thing I could do was sleep, I tried to keep my mind active by dodging from one thought to the next.

Had anyone seen Cynthia dragging me to her house? As preposterous as it seemed that a woman basically the same size as me could manage such a feat unseen, apparently was possible given the circumstances. Quickly surveying my neighbors, I knew the Bensons and Jungs would all be at work or school. Jo had left the day before to visit her daughters in Oklahoma City and the Patels were, of course, in India.

Had Peter decided to come home early? Was he concerned that my car was at home yet I was nowhere to be found? What would he do?

Where was the FBI when you needed them?

What if I didn't make it out of this situation? Although that was a path I knew I shouldn't travel, I wholeheartedly knew it was a possibility. My thoughts turned to Bobby and the yearning I often felt for him. A memory of holding Bobby near the end of his illness flooded through me. The pain that had pierced my heart during those last moments of his life overcame me once again. I didn't know what heaven would be like but had always hoped my mother's soul would be reunited with my child. I began to feel myself lulled into a near peaceful slumber, as I imagined myself tenderly holding my sweet little boy once again.

But that day is not today, I told myself as I shook my aching head. I still had a husband and daughter who I needed and who needed me. "I will survive this!" I told myself as I heard the lock begin to turn.

Victor stepped into the darkened room, reaching for the switch. He cursed under his breath when the light did not come on. As he stumbled over my first layer of obstacles, I pushed the cot forward knocking him off balance. As he staggered forward, I rushed out of the bunker closing the door behind me and came face to face with Cynthia. As she snarled at me, I opened a can of soda squirting it straight into her eyes. Then, taking the bra slung over my shoulder, hit her smack dab in the side of the head. Although it wasn't enough to knock her out, it definitely surprised and stunned her. As she staggered to regain her balance, I took advantage of the moment to push her aside and start climbing out of the storm shelter.

I was half way up the ladder, when someone grabbed my foot. Victor began to yank me back down into the shelter. Using my loose foot, I stepped on his hand as hard as I could. I began yelling "HELP" hoping there might be a neighbor nearby. No sooner had I cried out than another set of hands grabbed my legs. Losing my balance, I fell onto the floor of the shelter. Pain coursed through my arm and head as I felt myself being dragged back to my prison.

For the second time in a day, I was about to lose consciousness when I heard, "FBI!"

I recognized the sounds before I even opened my eyes. We had spent hours, days and months in hospitals with Bobby. The beeps of monitors, rolling of carts and muffled voices were all sounds I was too familiar with. As my eyes fluttered opened, I first saw Peter sleeping in a chair to the side of me, his hand covering mine. Although his eyes were closed, I could tell by his furrowed brow his was not a peaceful sleep. In the corner of the room, Lane was draped over a chair looking at her phone. For just a few seconds, I wanted to breathe in the same air as the two people I loved most in the world before I had to deal with the fall out of what had happened.

My slight movement alerted Lane as she looked up and with tears in her eyes said, "Mom!" Music to my ears. I turned to Peter who was smiling at me, also with tears in his eyes. Gently he squeezed my hand, "Ev."

I knew there was a lot of explaining to do, and I had lots of questions as well. For now, rest was what I needed, and fortunately, what the doctor ordered. Over the next twenty-four hours I drifted in and out of consciousness. I was quite aware of how my entire body ached. It wasn't until the second or third time that I surfaced out of my groggy state that I realized my arm was in a cast. Peter and Lane stood vigil the entire time. At one point, I thought Kevin was in the room, or was I dreaming?

By the following afternoon, I was allowed to have some Jell-O and broth. More awake than asleep at this point, I knew it was time to answer and ask questions.

"How did you find me?" I asked Peter.

"Kevin, or I guess I should say, Ben. I was confused when you were nowhere to be found when I got home. When I found your purse on the floor of the garage, I became worried so I started calling neighbors. No one had seen you. Fortunately, I decided to phone Kevin, Ben," he corrected himself.

"Just call him Kevin, it's easier," I assured him.

Giving me a strange look, he continued, "Kevin came over immediately and assessed the situation. He ordered me to come with him to his house where he pulled up surveillance video of the exterior of our house. It took a few minutes, but we caught footage of Cynthia dragging you out of the garage. I've got to tell you, Ev, that's got to be one of the strangest and most frightening things I've ever seen." Shaking his head, he continued, "Kevin grabbed a backpack and we headed to the Andersons'. We entered the garage just in time to hear what was apparently you falling. That's when Kevin pulled out a gun and yelled FBI."

"Talk about timing," I cautiously joked. "I guess you two have some questions,". Even in my semi-lucid state, I wasn't sure I had clearance to tell the entire story.

"Kevin has answered a few of them," Lane shared, "though most of his time, apparently, has been spent questioning Russian spies."

"If you tell me what you know, I can fill in the gaps," I wearily offered.

"We know the Andersons are Russian spies and Kevin is an FBI agent who you have apparently been working with. By what I saw in the ten minutes or so I was in Kevin's house, I'm assuming some of our other neighbors, including us, were suspected spies. How the heck did you get involved in this, Ev?" By the tone of his voice, I wasn't sure if he was annoyed, relieved or dumbfounded. I certainly appreciated his wide array of emotions. Afterall, I'd been experiencing them for weeks.

I slowly started to tell my story. After weeks of concealing so much, especially from Peter, it was cathartic to let it all out. I began with the series of incidents that had led me to reporting my suspicions about Kevin to the FBI. I could tell they were both shocked to hear 'the general's' death had been murder, perpetrated by Cynthia as it turned out.

"While you were in Barcelona, the FBI approached me about aiding in the investigation. They were impressed by my observation skills," I smiled at Lane. "In other words, your mom is nosy."

"I'm just thankful my mom is alive!" Lane stated emotionally. "I can't believe Kevin put you in this type of danger."

"You can't blame Kevin for what happened. Throughout this investigation, he has bent over backwards to protect me." I knew her anger towards Kevin was founded in more than his solicitation of my help. "We'll talk more about Kevin in a bit. First, I want to get my side of the story out."

"The last six weeks has just been a compilation of information I've gathered through casual and sometimes contrived conversations. I would report to Kevin and he would investigate. 'the general's' notebook is what caused everything to come to a head. Apparently, drainage issues caused by the Andersons' secret bunker was affecting the Walkers' yard. Bill's tenacity over making sure the issue was resolved is ultimately what got him killed. Poor Jo, I know this is going to add pain to an already broken heart," my voice drifted off.

"The Andersons weren't the only ones who were suspects," Peter urged me to continue.

"No, in the beginning there were six couples. As you know, we were included. Ties to the Whiteley Research Center is what got most people on the list of suspects. In our case, it was our relationship with Dmitry. Did you know he works with the Russian government to recruit international spies?" By the look on Peter's face, I was fairly certain he at the very least suspected it. This was definitely a conversation for another time.

"Through a variety of means, we were able to eliminate all but two couples, the Andersons and Jean and Randall." I could tell this shocked Lane.

"They are some of your closest friends," Lane said in an astonished voice. "Mom, how could you suspect them?"

"I didn't. At least not in the beginning. When I first started it was more about eliminating people I cared about from the board. But once you start down a path of deceit and suspicion, it's easy to become skeptical of everyone. Even people you love."

"The best spies are nice guys," Peter muttered under his breath.

Chapter 32

Thankfully, I was allowed to go home the next day. The doctor ordered a couple of weeks worth of rest, which right now sounded wonderful. Lane had arranged her schedule to work remotely, so I would have her company as I recuperated.

The front page of Deep Fork's paper featured a photo of a handcuffed Cynthia and Victor Anderson being led out of the county jailhouse by two FBI agents. There was no mention of Special Agent Benjamin Keith (Kevin) or myself in any of the accounts. Just as well, I thought.

> *"Deep Fork University, as well as our nation, are thankful for the foresightedness of the FBI in tracking down and apprehending these agents who posed a threat to our nation," Randall Weber, Deep Fork University President. "The important work done through the Whiteley Research Center and its DARPA affiliation will continue."*
>
> *A long-time neighbor, known to locals as Miss Essie, is quoted as saying, "How could she have been a spy? She had the most beautiful hydrangeas."*

As far as our neighbors and friends knew, I had taken a bad tumble during the rainstorm. Jean brought a casserole over ready to share everything she knew concerning the arrest of the Andersons.

"You know the aunt Cynthia was always visiting in St. Louis? She was actually a handler."

I truthfully was able to say I needed to rest, so Jean kept her visit short. But not before sharing, "You know, it's funny. If the FBI was going to suspect someone of being a Russian spy, I would have guessed it would have been me. After all, I'm the one with Russian roots." I watched as Jean crossed the street hoping she would never know how close her name was to the top of the list of suspects.

Kevin came over that evening to check on me, and I suspected, to begin to clear things up with Lane. Although I know he preferred to visit with me in private, the time for secrecy was over. I wanted Peter and Lane to be included in any conversation we might have. My days of keeping secrets from my family were behind me.

"Evelyn, I'm sorry for the way things went down," he sincerely shared. "Although we knew there was a propensity for violence with our suspects, I didn't anticipate such an overt act."

"Kevin, I guess I should call you Ben now. Ben, it was merely an unfortunate circumstance. If I had not surprised Cynthia in the garage, she probably would not have reacted so violently." I truly did not blame him for what was undoubtedly the most frightening moments of my life.

"I've been given permission to conduct your de-briefing interview in your home. I'll also need to collect the listening device Cynthia planted," Kevin said as he produced an evidence bag. Donning a pair of gloves, he retrieved the bug from under our dining room table. Both Peter and Lane looked shocked. Although they were aware of the big picture, neither one had realized the way our home, our sanctuary, had been violated.

"If you are up to it, I'll begin recording our conversation. I can also fill you in on missing pieces. After all, this investigation would not have wrapped up as quickly as it did without your help."

Ben turned on the recorder and I began telling, on the record, everything Cynthia had shared with me during my captivity. Apparently, she had not been as forthcoming in her FBI interrogation. I guess if you plan to kill your audience, you are a lot more talkative. Ben took notes throughout my narrative, stopping occasionally to ask questions.

"Your time with Victor was limited?" he asked.

"Very. When I awoke the first time, he was in the room and quite upset that Cynthia had abducted me. He ordered her not to do anything until he returned. Apparently, he had a meeting."

"With Randall," Peter interjected. "They were discussing the DARPA budget. Ironic isn't it?" he said dryly.

"The next time I saw Victor was when he entered the bunker and I attempted my escape."

"You know, you're becoming something of a legend in the Bureau. Your use of objects at your disposal for your escape, was impressive. They may need to add a session to our FBI training, Evelyn's Escape," he said with a smile. Turning to Peter he said, "From the moment I met Evelyn, I knew she was special. She has not disappointed."

Taking my hand, Peter smiled softly and said, "No argument from me." I had noticed Lane and Ben had not made eye contact since his arrival.

Evidently, Victor had been much more communicative in sharing information about his covert activities. His discomfort with Cynthia's activities had begun with the attack on Min. Cynthia had been in the research center placing a bug in the center's server. Unfortunately, Min had shown up unexpectedly. When she murdered 'the general', Victor became progressively agitated. Cynthia's increased visits to St. Louis had been to discuss this with her handler. Dmitry was called in to serve as a calming voice with Victor and remind him of the greater goal of his mission.

Out of the corner of my eye, I watched Peter as Ben spoke of Dmitry's role in this scenario. Peter had what one might call a 'poker face'. To the average person, you would not suspect him of anything, but I knew his 'tell'. The right corner of his mouth twitched slightly as Ben shared this information.

"So, what happens now?" I asked.

"Kirill Denisov and Vera Yerzova will be charged with espionage and moved to a federal penitentiary. In cases like this, there are often deals and trades made, so it's hard to tell what their final fate will be.

"Cynthia is a murderer. She must be held accountable for Bill's murder," I was appalled to think this might not happen.

"The fact that she confessed this to you is important. Although Victor claims she committed the murder, your account confirms it. Hopefully, your statement will carry enough weight to negate any 'trade' made with the Russians, at least for Cynthia. Victor's research knowledge makes him the most valuable asset of the two of them. Evelyn you had already observed Cynthia's resentment of Victor's success. It seems her perceived secondary role in their relationship is what triggered this aggressive side of her."

As Ben stood to leave, he turned to Lane and asked, "Can we talk?" The two of them grabbed coats and stepped onto the back veranda. Ben lit a fire in the firepit and took a seat beside Lane. Peter suggested we retreat to the bedroom. I suspect not only because we were exhausted but also to give Lane and Ben the space and time needed to figure out where they would go from here.

I must say nothing feels as good as climbing into your own bed, especially after such a physically and emotionally draining forty-eight hours. I carefully positioned myself on my side with my casted arm resting on a pillow. Peter crawled into bed gently covering my good hand with his. We laid in silence for a few minutes, each of us reflecting on the turn our lives had taken. I finally broke the silence with a thought that had been nagging at me.

"You know all my secrets. Don't you think it's time to tell me yours?"

A fleeting look of surprise went over his face and then he smiled, "You're good, Ev. When did you know?"

"Your mouth was twitching when Kevin, I mean Ben, was talking about Dmitry."

"My story is not nearly as dramatic as yours. Just so you know, the CIA has given me clearance to talk about this with you."

Although a part of me should have guessed Peter's participation would be with the CIA, I knew my face still registered surprise.

"Six years ago, when I was in Italy, the CIA approached me. Like the FBI, my connection with Dmitry was the trigger. The difference was instead of making me a suspect, I was targeted as someone who might be able to glean information. They recruited me to consciously grow my relationship with Dmitry. Whether you have been aware of it or not, my overseas trips now always include contact with my Russian friend."

"Inviting him and his wife to join us in Greece is part of your assignment?" I asked already knowing the answer.

"I still consider Dmitry a friend, but yes there is an ulterior motive. I'm not sure anything I've reported to the CIA has been of any consequence. At least not until his recent visit. I immediately contacted the agency and was ordered to keep a timeline and narrative of all of Dmitry's moves and contacts. Especially in regard to his interest in the DARPA project."

The two of us laid silent for a long time, each lost in our own thoughts.

"I didn't like keeping it from you, Ev. But I think given your recent experience, you understand why I did."

"I recognize why each of us accepted the assignments we did. But like you, I felt uncomfortable with the secrecy. We are stronger together than apart."

"So, what are you saying, Ev?" Peter looked a little perplexed.

"In the future, we work as a couple." I wasn't sure what that might include, but I knew no matter what, I wanted Peter by my side.

Debbie Williams

Epilogue

In just a few hours, I would be boarding a flight to join Peter in Istanbul. Reading through my to do list I noted I still had several last-minute chores to take care of before heading to the airport. As I stepped onto the front porch to give my geraniums a hefty drink of water, I scanned my street. It was hard to believe four months had passed since the arrest of Cynthia and Victor.

As predicted by FBI Agent Ben Keith (I still thought of him as Kevin), a deal was in fact brokered, but only for Victor. He returned to Russia and where, I assumed, he would continue to pursue his scientific interests. Cynthia, on the other hand, was sentenced to life imprisonment for the murder of Bill Walker. Although my statement was included in the case against her, in the end Victor had spilled his guts and, in fact, turned over the murder weapon, a tactical flashlight. I'm not sure if Victor had a premonition where this might go, but he had secretly stored it making sure Cynthia's fingerprints and 'the general's' blood was intact. Nice guys might make the best spies, but as Miss Essie would say, "There is no honor among thieves."

For several weeks after the arrest, our neighborhood had been quite a tourist attraction as people drove by the Spy House. Needless to say, the neighborhood gossip centered around the investigation and arrest. Although the undercover FBI agent was never identified, it did not take a rocket scientist to figure out it was Kevin Crank. Within forty-eight hours of the Anderson's arrest, he had vacated his house. Recently a young couple had purchased and moved into the property. As per the neighborhood's tradition, I delivered cookies as a welcome gift. Anxious to give me a tour and share their remodeling dreams, I was able to catch a glimpse of the bedroom that had served as the FBI Command Post. The window had been uncovered but the bookshelves were intact. I wondered at what point the new owners might discover the closet hidden behind the shelves.

Jo had taken the news of Bill's murder better than I'd anticipated. Although it was upsetting, she expressed how satisfied he would have been to know his patrol unearthed a Russian Sleeper Cell. She had put her house on the market last week and was preparing to move to Oklahoma City to be near her daughters. I completely understood her need for a new environment after such a profound loss. After all, that is exactly what brought Peter, Lane and me to Deep Fork twenty years ago.

The third house that would be changing ownership was of course the Andersons'. Seized by the FBI as an asset forfeiture, they had spent nearly three months combing through the house and hidden bunker's contents. Only recently had it been released to be sold. Naturally, the neighborhood's gossip mill had a lot of speculation as to what would happen with the proceeds of the sale. Because I had an inside track with the FBI, I knew an announcement would be made in the next week indicating proceeds would go to our local police department to help fund and support neighborhood watch programs, an acknowledgment to 'the general's' role in the case.

Although Ben had left the neighborhood, he was not out of our lives. After completing the Deep Fork assignment, he took a field office position in Dallas. Lane shared with us they were planning to take a cautious approach to their relationship. I'm not quite sure what that meant, but Peter and I agreed we needed to keep our distance from them as a couple until they knew where they were going. Lane continued her periodic visits with us, but our talk about Ben and their relationship was quite limited. Although at times I thought my brain might burst with questions, I vowed to respect her judgment and feelings.

As I finished caring for my plants and moved inside, I was once again reminded of Scout's reflection from *To Kill a Mockingbird*, "that you really never know a man until you stand in his shoes and walk around in them." Through my role in the FBI investigation, I had learned of the troubling and difficult background of Sofia and Gary and the fear that had overshadowed the Jungs for years. To say nothing of the sordid world of spies and the toll a covert lifestyle can take on an FBI Agent.

Now it was time for me to begin a new journey. This time, my partner in crime would be my partner in life, Peter. We had agreed to continue the CIA's directive to grow our relationship with Dmitry. Our Russian friend and his wife would be joining us for five days in Greece. It would be an interesting dance. Peter and I were briefed to assume Dmitry was aware of my kidnapping by Cynthia. He would not, however, know about my participation in the FBI investigation. What intel might be gathered was unclear, our orders were simply to maintain a positive and close relationship with Dmitry.

I took one last glance in the mirror as I closed my suitcase. The reflection looking back was definitely not that of a twenty-five-year-old. What I did see was a mature woman confident in who she was and what she could accomplish when put to the test. I also saw a woman who had experienced deep sorrow but surfaced on the other side a kinder, more compassionate soul. Perhaps not as naïve as I had once been but certainly not cynical which was important because after all, the best spies are nice guys.

ABOUT THE AUTHOR

Debut author, Debbie Williams, has spent her entire professional career creating fertile and creative learning environments. For over twenty years she worked in the field of early childhood education first as a public-school teacher and ultimately as the director of an early childhood center. In 2011, along with a band of dedicated women, she helped to envision and open a children's museum.

Much like the protagonist in *The Neighborhood*, she is embarking on a new career later in life. Okay, maybe not as an FBI Asset, but as an author. After retiring, she decided it was time to get the story that had been tumbling around in her mind for twenty years onto paper.

In the words of Miss Essie, *The Neighborhood's* matriarch, "*Never be afraid to try something new. Remember, amateurs built the ark; professionals built the Titanic.*"

Made in the USA
Monee, IL
09 November 2021